The Deck Never Lies

A Mystery with a Tarot Twist

Joyce Bennett-Hall

Published by

ISBN:
ISBN-13: 979-8-218-74337-6

DEDICATION

This book is dedicated to:

My Mastermind partner and friend, Angela Overby.

Robert Barrango and Linda Rhoho who fielded the story for me.

My granddaughter, Amy Tunnermann, for developing the characters with me.

Adriann Santer for bringing the cover to life with your art and for being a true kindred spirit.

Jesse Valenzulea, for his constant encouragement and support.

Dr. James Mellon, for inspiring me to stretch beyond my reach.

Shawn Hall, for the many gifts he has given me.

CHAPTER 1

Under a dark, indigo, cloud-covered sky dotted with a colony of gulls, a small fishing boat rides the early morning waves. A tinge of red comes through the clouds, indicating the sun will be making an appearance soon. It was a picture-perfect morning with the ocean waves embracing the little boat as if they were protecting it from some unforeseen sea monster. The squawking from above became melodic. The gulls seemed to be singing, *"This way, the fish are this way."*

"Listen to them birds. It's gonna be a good day. They're tellin' us we'll make our quota. I feel it in my bones. Again, listen to them gulls. We ain't had this kind of an escort in a long time," Arnie said in his gravelly voice.

"So, now you understand gull talk, huh? Maybe it's just your arthritis kicking up," Tom said teasingly.

"Yep. I understand them. Been on these waters a long time. They're showing us the way."

"What if they are following us for the fish? Did you think of that?"

"If they were pelicans, maybe so. Not gulls."

"I still say it's your arthritis kicking up."

For much of the last one hundred years, San Pedro and Terminal Island, in California, were home to the largest fishing industry in the United States. In 1937, the San Pedro fishing fleet numbered nearly five hundred boats. Today, the fleet is down to less than a few dozen boats. Arnie's boat is one of the last remaining ones.

Arnie Lund is a stout man with all the looks of a sea captain, minus the peg leg. He adorns a scruffy mustache and an untrimmed beard and wears a bucket hat that hasn't seen soap in years. He looks to be in his late seventies, but the truth of the matter is Arnie is probably somewhere in his early sixties. Arnie took over his family business and has been running his small boat for over thirty years.

"So, Tom, how's that lawyering coming along?"

"Arnie, I still have to graduate and then pass the bar exam before I can do any lawyering."

Tom Hart is in his last year of law school and helps Arnie out on short fishing jaunts. He has loved going down to the docks ever since his dad took him and his sister, Ann, to watch the oil tankers and fishing boats come into port. Tom was thrilled when he met Arnie on the docks one day, and that meeting developed into a job on Arnie's fishing boat. He loves going out on their fishing excursions because it gives him time to clear his head from all the studying and Arnie appreciates his help.

Tom stands a little over six feet tall and weighs around 220 pounds with hair just a shade less than a carrot. Both he and Ann inherited the red hair from their mom's side of the family. "Carrot Top" and "Red" were the names he and Ann had to live with all through school.

The crew of four men started betting on the size of the haul, a game they played each time they went out to sea. Tom said he felt it was going to be the biggest haul yet this week.

"Tom, you say that every time we go out. Wishful thinking, my boy, wishful thinking," Arnie said laughing, which caused him to start coughing. "Damn cigarettes."

"I thought you were going to quit those?"

"Nah. Probably be smokin' at my funeral." Arnie put his hand over his eyes, looked around and continued. "We're out far enough now so let's anchor and prepare to cast off the net and see who wins the bet today."

The anchor was dropped, and each man took his place, picked up a section of the net and flung it out. Even though Tom has been helping on and off for about a year and has cast many a net, he still gets a thrill each time he lets go and watches it fly out to sea. It's like a flying saucer coming in for a landing and disappearing under the water. As the net sank below the surface, the gulls no longer seemed interested and continued on their way.

That tinge of red was getting brighter, allowing the rays of the upcoming sun to shine through. Pelicans, loons, and other various sea birds entertained their audience on the meager fishing boat bobbing in the sea. As the men waited to see what their first haul would be, they went about the chore of getting ready for what they hoped would be an abundance of fish.

Ropes started indicating that the net was ready to be brought up for emptying. As the net started up it became noticeably heavier than usual. The retrieval clamp stalled with the net halfway up out of the water.

"Man, what the hell is in this net? It sure looks like we caught something bigger than a school of fish. We'll have to manually bring it up."

As the men struggled to bring the net out of the water, there were a lot of grunts and groans. Sweating and breathing hard one of the men noticed that the clamp that closes the net was half open.

"It's half open. No wonder the net isn't coming up. The retrieval clamp malfunctioned. What a bummer."

"It shouldn't have, it's fairly new. Guys, I know this sucks, but we're gonna have to finish with good old manpower."

With a chorus of grunting and groaning, the men continued trying to lift the net out of the water. Muscles bulged and quivered under the strain. One man slipped and stumbled.

"Damn," he grunted as his knees buckled, but he refused to

let go. And then it began to rise. The weight shifted one inch, then another, but it felt like the ocean was trying to keep it for its own.

Finally, after stopping several times to catch their breath and with calloused hands, the men hauled the net up and swung it over and onto the deck. A triumphant roar could be heard but stopped abruptly when they watched half of the fish spill out and saw the thing that caused the malfunction.

"What the hell?" Tom reached for his phone.

CHAPTER 2

"Hey Cowboy."

"Why, if it isn't the esteemed Ann Hart. I should have known you'd be here. Who called you?"

"Tom. He was out with Arnie on a morning fishing trip and called me when they pulled in their haul."

"Well, it's good to see you even if it is under these circumstances. Over dinner would have been better."

Waving a fly away, Ann ignored the last part. "So, what happened here? Tom said their net caught a body of a young woman."

"That's right. A young woman who looks to have been killed and dumped into the ocean. The coroner is with her now."

They stood on the dock embraced by the morning sun. The water sparkled in the sunlight, creating a kaleidoscope of colors. The air was filled with the smell of fish as fishing boats were arriving to unload their haul for the day.

Detective Hank Johnson, Cowboy, as Ann calls him, left Albuquerque two years ago to further his career in a larger city. Since he joined the force, he has made quite a name for himself. He has become one of the city's top homicide detectives. Detective Johnson has also become well known for his Western attire. He sports a Stetson, a vest, boots, and his piercing blue eyes match the turquoise in his bolo tie.

Hank grew up on a working ranch in Socorro, New Mexico. After his parents died in a truck accident, he sold the ranch, enrolled in the police academy and the rest is history.

Ann Hart, besides being Tom's older sister, is a Criminal Investigator who holds a PI license. The Private Investigator license allows her to carry a weapon and since most of her work is for law enforcement, she feels safer knowing she has her Smith & Wesson.

She rarely does independent investigative work unless it is a follow-up for an attorney or she's writing something for one of the newspapers for which she has received some journalism awards. Ann has worked with Detective Johnson on several occasions, and they have what you call a coquettish relationship.

Her reddish auburn hair is complemented by her green eyes and is one of her striking features. She hates it when Detective Hank Johnson calls her "Red," which he does at times just to tease her. Ann is smart and sharp-witted and can hold her own with Detective Johnson.

When Tom called Ann about the girl's body, she wasn't really surprised. The card she pulled from her tarot deck during her morning ritual was the Ten of Swords. The Ten of Swords is not a good omen. It can represent backstabbing, betrayal, badmouthing, bitching behind your back, bitterness, and enemies. It is a card of failure, ruin, collapse, severing ties, goodbyes, and the final nail in the coffin of a relationship or situation. After Tom's call, she jumped in her 1995 Alfa Romero Spider convertible, she named Empress, and drove immediately to the docks.

Hank and Ann started walking down to the end of the dock. In the bright sunlight the dock felt alive with color and sound. A gentle breeze stirred in the air ruffling Ann's hair. Hank took his hand and gently pushed her hair back into place. When they reached the end of the dock, the body was just being covered by the coroner.

Upon questioning him, they found out that the young woman appeared to have died from drowning and probably had been in the water less than 48 hours. He added that there appeared to be a large bump on the back of her head and some sort of puncture wound at the base of her neck. He would know more after the results of the forensic autopsy.

"So, Red, can I buy you a cup of coffee?"

"If a Danish is included, the answer is yes."

She met Hank at a coffee shop not far from the docks. They ordered their coffee and found a small table outside away from the crowd of people. Hank asked what Ann was up to these past few months. Ann and Hank worked on their last caper together several months back. She caught him up to date and asked about him as well. They did their usual small talk, always skirting around Hanks's obvious attraction to her.

"So, you once told me that you do some quirky thing every morning. Do you still do that 'thing'?" Hank asked.

Ann, laughing, answered, "If you mean my morning ritual, the answer is yes."

"So, what exactly is it again?"

"Well, if you must know, I start my day by meditating and then I pull a Tarot card or sometimes I meditate on the card I pull. It's like a compass telling me the direction of the day."

"A card can tell you the direction of the day, hmm. Can it tell you what the weather is going to be like as well?" Hank added, somewhat sarcastically.

"As a matter of fact, sometimes it can. You sound like a skeptic. Do you have a morning ritual?"

"Sure, hit the snooze button on the alarm a couple of times, make coffee when I do get up which I take with me to the bathroom while I shower, then drink it, get dressed, and out the door I go," Hank answered.

"Really?"

"Nah, kidding. I only hit the snooze button once." They both laughed and then went back to the conversation about the young woman whose body was found.

"I think she was killed on a boat and thrown overboard not

too far out," Ann said.

"You may be right. What little clothing she had left on indicated that it might have been a dress. Maybe something you women wear to a party. I don't think she was out on a fishing boat. Although, she could have been on one of those tour boats."

"Maybe, but if she was killed and thrown off one of those, someone would have seen that happening. I think once we have more information about her, we need to check out all the bigger private boats that may have been hosting a party on Saturday," Ann suggested.

"What do you mean, 'we'?" Detective Johnson retorted. "You know the routine. As I find out the information, I will include you when appropriate. I swear, you should've become a detective."

"No, you detectives are too stuffy and must follow too many damn rules. You know I'm not a conformist. I like the freedom of doing things my way when following up on a lead. Thanks for being willing to share information with me. I appreciate that. And in return, I'll share what I find out as well, if appropriate."

Hank just laughed. He loved her sense of humor. He knew the truth of the matter was she was a damn good investigator and helped him on more than one occasion. He held a soft spot in his heart for her ever since he learned that her mother had died at the hand of a stray bullet.

Ann's mom just happened to be in the wrong place at the wrong time. From what he gathered from the reports, he learned that her mother was in a neighborhood food mart when the store was overtaken by several armed men who apparently intended to rob the store. Whatever they were going to do was thwarted by the owner, who had a gun. The owner said when he pulled his gun out from under the counter, one of the robbers saw it and started shooting at him. So, he shot back. One of the bullets hit Ann's mom and immediately killed her.

When the shooting stopped, both the owner and robber

had been hit. The other men fled the scene as soon as they heard the sirens of the police. All the men were eventually caught and arrested. The owner of the store survived. The shooter did not. Ann and her brother Tom were raised by their father ever since.

CHAPTER 3

✦⁺✦ THREE WEEKS EARLIER ✦⁺✦

"Bob, can you pick me up in a half hour? I'd like to have a meeting with you and Stan about the numbers from our last film," Stephen Knoll asked. "You can? Great, see you outside in a bit."

Bob Kerry has been Stephen Knoll's manager ever since Stephen's lucky break which got him into the film industry. Stephen has had four consecutive successful films, mostly due to Bob's marketing ability. Agents like Bob Kerry were rare. He's assertive, not aggressive and has the gift of persuasion. He was able to negotiate quite a lucrative package for Stephen's last production.

Stan Ritkowski is Stephen's accountant. He has also been with Stephen Knoll since the beginning of his career. He tries to keep Stephen's accounts in order and it's quite a job since Stephen likes to spend money on extravagant things. The last spending spree he went on, he wanted to buy an eighty-foot yacht. Stan talked him out of it by explaining to Stephen all the fees associated with the yacht. Those fees, as well as the cost of a crew, would put a real dent in his portfolio. It would put more than a dent. To put it in Stan's words, "Stephen that yacht, instead of riding the waves on the ocean could lead you down the road to the poorhouse." Stephen got the point and decided not to go forward with purchasing the yacht.

On the way to Stan's office, Stephen asked Bob what he thought of the idea of a celebration. Bob listened and queried the reason for the celebration. Stephen explained that he wanted to celebrate the success of their last film.

"Do you think Stan is going to go for my idea?" Stephen asked.

"Well, he may hit the ceiling after your last celebratory idea."

"You mean the yacht?"

"Yes, the yacht. He just about had a stroke."

"Well, that's where I want to have the celebration, on a yacht."

"What yacht? You didn't...."

"No, no, of course not. I didn't go out and buy a yacht. After the last speech about money from Stan, there would be no way. I don't think I could sit through another one of his money speeches. I was thinking about renting one. What do you think?"

"Well, if renting one doesn't lead you down the road to the poor house."

"Ha, ha, very funny."

Bob and Stephen pulled up in front of a sleek, modern building boasting its large windows and canopied entrance. A middle-aged man, wearing a red cap and blue vest, approached the parked car and greeted Bob.

"Good day, Sir."

"Yes, it is. And good day to you as well."

Bob gave the keys to the man in a red cap and blue vest and walked behind Stephen into the building. As they entered the elevator, someone called out Stephen's name.

"Stephen Knoll! Loved your last film."

Stephen gave a thank you nod and waved as he entered the elevator next to Bob.

"It never gets old, does it?"

"No, it doesn't. I love hearing accolades from movie goers."

When the elevator doors slid open on the 10th floor, Stan was already standing there, looking like a museum docent waiting for a tour group. He held a notepad, which never seemed to leave his hands.

Stephen, being caught off guard, asked, "What the hell, Stan? What are you doing out here in the hallway?" Before Stan could answer, Stephen continued, "Let's go in your office. I've got a great idea I want to talk to you about."

Stan embarrassed, said, "Of course. I was just walking back to my office when I heard the elevator and figured it might be you guys."

What he didn't say was that he had a visitor. Someone who he hustled out of the office the moment he heard the elevator ding, making sure that they weren't seen.

Stephen didn't acknowledge what Stan said and just walked into his office. Stan's office was furnished with an oversized walnut desk with carefully placed piles of neatly stacked papers. A brown couch sat in front of the desk with two matching chairs on either side. Bookshelves filled with accounting and law books lined the wall behind the desk. The floor-to-ceiling windows, the kind that give one vertigo, were on the far side of the room.

Bob walked over to the couch while avoiding looking towards the windows and Stephen sat down next to Bob, took in a deep breath, and began his pitch for a party.

"So, Stan, I want to have a celebration on a yacht. You know, to enjoy our successes from the last four films. Invite all the people that helped make the film a success...."

Stan interrupted Stephen, and said, in a sarcastic tone, "Really?"

"Now, don't get your balls in an uproar. I don't want to buy a yacht...I want to rent a yacht. I know someone, who knows someone, who has a yacht and rents it out with a crew and all. I already talked to the guy who owns the yacht, and he loves my films."

"So does that mean he will rent it to you with a big discount because he loves your films?" he said with a little less sarcasm this time.

Stephen ignored Stan's question and continued telling the guys what he wanted.

Stan asked, "Bob what do you think?"

"Well, I think if we could keep the cost reasonable it would be great publicity."

Stan spoke up again. "Just make sure you stay within this financial range," he said, giving him the budget that he had quickly jotted down.

Stephen nodded and agreed. The meeting continued where notes were taken, plans were made, lists were written, and at the end of the meeting, the celebration was a go.

CHAPTER 4

✦ ✦ TWO WEEKS EARLIER ✦ ✦

"Francine, have you responded to Stephen Knoll's invite yet?"

"No. Damn, I keep putting it off. The truth of the matter is that I am really pissed that he is hosting a party, especially on a yacht, without calling me for my help."

"Don't go cutting off your nose to spite your face. If you don't go, people will think it's sour grapes. Just think of all the networking you can do. Call him!" Francine's assistant said in a firm tone.

"I will. I will. I will call him today." Francine walked across the large living room, known as the entertainment room, plunking one of the keys on her grand piano, as she walked towards the brocade couch. Feeling a wave of jealousy, she sat down, picked up her phone off the arm of the couch, where she had left it, and dialed Stephen.

Francine Brittone is one of Hollywood's most famous socialites and is known as the "party giver." Francine is a big woman with a matching personality, the kind that sucks the air out of a room. Anyone who is someone in the film industry knows Francine and tries to get in her good graces. If someone is lucky enough to do so, they have a good shot at getting attention from casting directors on any new and upcoming film project.

"Hey, Stephen, this is Francine calling to RSVP to your party. I wouldn't miss it for the world. I will be there with bells on." She left her message and placed her phone back on the arm of the

14

couch.

"Stephen Knoll sure has been a lucky sort. Four box office hits. He's a great catch for some young lady."

"Well, with his money and looks, he can afford to play the field," Francine's assistant answered.

"It is odd I've never seen a picture of him with any women."

"Maybe he's one of those milk toast kind of guys."

"You mean gay?"

"Yes."

"No, I don't think so. Stephen is cast as a leading man and heartthrob in his movies, and he sure does play that part well. I wouldn't mind being his leading lady, even if it was just once. Well, enough of this now, I did call and leave a message that I would be attending. "Can't wait," she said under her breath.

CHAPTER 5

In a small Santa Monica Bistro, overlooking the ocean, Courtney Hill and two friends were discussing the upcoming yacht gala. A server, standing nearby, seemed impatient, waiting to get the sign that the girls were ready to order. She was wearing the traditional French Bistro waiter uniform, black pants, black vest, white blouse, and a scarf loosely tied around her neck in place of a black bow tie. She looked over at the girls once again, but still they showed no sign.

"What are you going to wear to Stephen's party?" Courtney Hill asked her two friends.

"I'm so excited about this party. I never thought I would be going to a movie star's yacht for any reason, let alone a party," Jill Huffer replied.

"I know, right?" I'm going to wear my long green sleeveless dress. Casual dressy," Lisa Crane responded to Courtney's question.

"Oh, that sounds nice. I'm going to wear a long blue paisley dress, with long yellow beads," Courtney said. "Jill, you didn't answer."

"Hawaiian is what I thought. I'm going to wear a sarong dress that's black with gold print flowers and gold thongs."

"Sounds lovely, Jill." Courtney responded.

Courtney Hill is the daughter of Holly Hill a well-known film porn star. Her father is Mark Hill, a Beverly Hills corporate attorney. Holly and Mark have been separated for several years because of her chosen profession. Courtney lives with her father and has

16

recently graduated from an arts college. She aspires to become an actor, and has had several bit parts, including a small part in one of Stephen Knoll's pictures. Since then, the tabloids have described her as the new and upcoming star. Courtney seems to have made it big from a small part. Courtney caught Stephen's eye, and he has been smitten with her ever since.

Jill Huffer has been one of Courtney's best friends since grade school. Like Courtney, she grew up with a father who practices law, though in a different specialty. Jill's father, Carl, is a defense attorney and works in an office in Encino 20 miles from downtown Los Angeles. Jill's mother, Donna, is a court reporter. Jill works for her dad as an intern as she is in her final leg of law school.

Lisa Crane is also a best friend of Courtney's. They met in drama class in high school and have been friends ever since. Lisa has her sights set on the theatre and has performed with some local groups. Her dream is to be on Broadway. Her parents, Mason and Amelia, are both in real estate.

"Courtney, thanks so much for inviting us to come along with you to the party. I know that your invitation was for you and plus one, so I hope plus two doesn't present a problem for you."

"You know I don't go anywhere social without my two besties. "Plus two" will not be a problem, I have an 'in' with Stephen."

"What kind of 'in' do you mean? Are we hearing there is a secret romance going on?"

"Yes, tell us."

"You guys are funny. No, there is no 'thing' here. No secret romance or any other kind of romance going on. Since I appeared in one of his movies, he has made a special point of talking to me when I'm on the set. It is flattering, that is all."

"Alright, but be careful. It sounds like he may have more on his mind than just flattering you."

Courtney just laughed and said, "It's getting late, I think we need to order lunch."

"Yes, I think that is a good idea."

"I may be too excited to eat," Jill said. "Oh, I just can't wait for the yacht party. It is going to be so much fun."

CHAPTER 6

Hany Al Shariff is an investor who believed in Stephen Knoll when others were leery. Stephen was an unknown commodity, and investors were not willing to put their money behind his project. Hany Al Shariff had a nose for box office hits, and he was sure Stephen had a box office hit. He invested his time as well as his money. He excelled in scouting the talent and ended up helping both Bob and Stan manage the production costs. It all paid off for everyone involved.

Hany became family to Stephen due to the amount of time they spent together. His siblings are still in Lebanon and will remain. Their parents were killed during the Lebanese war, and as a result he and his siblings were displaced for a while. After some time, they were able to salvage most of their things, relocate, and resettle as a family. After some time, Hany decided to come to America and was drawn to the glitz and glamour of the Hollywood scene.

Hany Al Shariff's family and friends financially funded his move and invested in a home in Beverly Hills. He didn't skip a beat and fell right into the lifestyle, earning him a place in society circles. People saw him more prestigious and financially well-off than he really was. That got him into the doors where he was able to raise both into alignment with his perceived persona.

He started to raise money for films in the can, films that were made and then just shelved. Hany hit it lucky with one of the films. It became a number one box office hit after sitting in the can for quite some time. He met Stephen Knoll at the premiere of that movie. When Stephen talked to him about his project, Hany Al

Shariff knew that with the right talent and management, Stephen could have a winner.

Hany spent most of his time at the studios, hoping to spot new talent. He would watch auditions and filming for independent producers. One particular day, he strolled over to a set where they were shooting a movie when he saw Courtney delivering her lines. He was struck by how naturally beautiful she was. Standing in the back, watching the shoot, he knew he had found the right talent for Stephen's next film. Even though she only had a bit part, she delivered her lines with ease. Hany waited until they were finished shooting, then walked towards Courtney.

Hany introduced himself to Courtney and shared his interest in her for a new upcoming film. Lisa Crane happened to be on the set that day to give Courtney moral support, as this was Courtney's first film. Lisa made sure she introduced herself to Hany and even flirted with him a bit. When Hany didn't show any interest in engaging with her, she reluctantly settled her hormones down.

Once Hany explained his role in finding talent for Stephen Knoll, she agreed to meet with him and Stephen to discuss the project. Courtney heard Mr. Knoll's name mentioned around the studios and felt comfortable agreeing to the meeting.

The meeting did take place, and as the saying goes, *the rest is history.*

CHAPTER 7

✦ NIGHT OF THE YACHT PARTY ✦

As Lisa Crane zipped up her long green dress, she stepped in front of the mirror and exclaimed, "Looking good, Lisa. You should turn some heads tonight!" She slipped her low-heeled shoes on, matching her dress, of course, and adorned herself with a long coral bead necklace. She stepped back in front of the mirror and said, "Yep, looking good. You will be turning some heads tonight."

Lisa loves the stage. Even though she has been in some local theatre groups, there has not been much action for her over the last year. She tried out for several parts, only to lose out to other girls. When she and Courtney were in the same drama class, the scouts mostly invited Courtney to try out for parts. Lisa has always felt second best to Courtney in every area of her life.

When they first started school, all the boys made over Courtney, and that continued right up to and through college. Many nights, Lisa sat home when Courtney was out having fun on a date. The day she went to the studio to support Courtney she saw Hany Al Shariff eyeing Courtney and got a twinge of jealousy. Then he had her cast in Stephen Knoll's film project. Although she was happy for her friend on the one hand, she was envious on the other. She started going down that rabbit hole, "Why does Courtney get all the breaks?"

Tonight, all she could think about was having fun at the yacht party. Tonight, she was happy that her friend got the break. She thought, *maybe tonight will be my break.*

CHAPTER 8

Excited about going to the yacht party, Jill Huffer hurried home from her dad's office to get ready. She usually didn't work on Saturday; however, she needed to finish a research project for school.

Jill is in her last year of law school and will be graduating in just a few months. Studying for the bar exam, which she plans to take right after graduation, has taken up most of her time. Not much time for parties. David, Jill's boyfriend, has been helping Jill study for the exam and even their dates have come down to nights of studying, pizza, and beer.

Jill met David Wesberg in law school. She and David started dating during her second year and his third. Since then, David graduated, passed the bar exam, and has recently joined a law firm that represents small business owners.

Jill is looking forward to the day that she and David can spend more time together. In fact, she is hoping that they will get married, even though David hasn't given her any indication of an awaiting proposal. She is hoping once he gets settled into his new job and she graduates, the subject will come up. David has been sensing her anticipation of a proposal, but David has a secret. A secret that prevents him from meeting her expectations. A secret that could cost him his career. A secret that someone has just found out.

CHAPTER 9

Calm waters, clear night, and balmy weather. Perfect evening for a yacht party. Limousines, luxury sports cars, and a smattering of other priceless cars pulled up in front of the valet, while many others parked in an adjacent lot. Courtney, Lisa, and Jill arrived in a limousine provided and paid for by Stephen Knoll, followed by a modest car driven by David, Jill's boyfriend. He decided not to ride with the girls, so they would have their special time together. He eventually joined them, and together they entered the water taxi to embark on the evening's celebration. A lone man joined them in the boat.

Courtney's parents, Mark and Holly, came separately, of course. Mark drove up in a modest car, and Holly came in a snazzy sports car that was driven by quite a handsome gentleman, probably one of her co-stars. Shortly afterwards, Lisa's parents arrived followed by Jill's.

More people arrived, dressed in a variety of fashionable boat wear. Women in long casual dresses to shorts with sequin tops, and everything in between. Hawaiian shirts were abundant on the men, with a few conservative dress shirts covered up with sportscoats. It was a salad of clothing, for sure.

The water taxis went back and forth all evening and well into the night. From the amplified sounds brought ashore by the water, it was apparent the celebration was a success. People came and went until, finally, the lights flickered, signaling that the party was over. The final water taxi dropped off the last group of people...all but one.

CHAPTER 10

Ann heard her phone ping, indicating that she received a message or notification of some sort. When she looked at her phone, she smiled and felt a bit of a tingle. It was a text from Detective Hank Johnson asking her to meet him. She waited a couple of seconds before she texted back saying she would.

"Thanks Red, for meeting me for lunch. Although, I would have preferred dinner."

Ann smiled, rolled her eyes a bit, and then replied, "I did some checking, and there was a yacht that was rented several days ago for an offshore party. And guess who rented it?"

"Stephen Knoll, the movie producer, and actor. I know, I got the report from one of my people yesterday."

"Okay Cowboy, were you going to share that information with me?"

"Yes, I just did."

Ann and Hank bantered back and forth about the information that he hadn't shared earlier for a bit longer. Ann convinced him to let her see the guest list once he obtained it. Hank knew how important it was to Ann to be part of the investigation into the death of the young woman. The truth of the matter was, he liked having her around. Hank also knew people are more apt to talk more freely to someone other than a detective. People have secrets they would rather not have the police know.

Hank went on to say, "We think we know who the young woman was. Just waiting for confirmation from one of our medical personnel."

"Who was she?" Ann asked.

"We think her name is Courtney Hill, the young starlet who was in Stephen Knoll's latest film."

"If it is Courtney Hill, I would like to go with you to talk with the parents."

"Once they are notified, and we go through our procedures of identification, I give you my word, when I go to follow up with them, you can tag along. I will let them know that you are helping the department with the investigation on behalf of their daughter."

"Really? You are asking for my help?"

"Yes Red, I am asking, unless you are too busy?"

"Cowboy, you are too funny. Of course, I want to be part of this investigation, and what took you so long to ask? Seriously, I really do appreciate you including me. For the record, I knew you would."

"I'm not going to ask how you knew because I don't want to hear that the cards told you so."

"Ok, since you don't want to know, I won't tell you that the cards did. And I won't tell you the card was the King of Swords."

"Of course the cards did. What was I thinking? Although I like being a King," Chuckled Hank. "You can start calling me Your Highness."

"Really? In your dreams," Ann retorted.

They joked around with each other for a few more minutes, then Hank popped in and said, "In any case, you are the best. I could use your help on this one, since I don't have a field team on this case. If this young woman was killed on the yacht during the time of the party, there will be a lot of people to interview. I will know more when we get all the information from the medical personnel."

Ann continued to speculate with Hank as to how Courtney, if that is who she turns out to be, was killed. It seemed likely that she was killed at the Stephen Knoll yacht party. Ann was anxious to sink her teeth into this investigation. Solving problems or mysteries fueled her, and Hank knew that as well.

She got her curiosity and tenacity from her father. Michael Hart was a corporate investigator. He investigated some of the major corporations around the country that were suspected of fraud, copyright infringement, and or cyber-criminal activity. Michael was a brilliant investigator and could separate the 'the wheat from the chaff' rapidly. At times, he was hired by private individuals who were considering partnerships and mergers.

When Michael's wife was killed in a robbery gone wrong, he didn't have time to wallow in his grief. He had two children who needed him and quickly stepped into the role of a single parent. He learned how to juggle parenting with work, which didn't leave much time for anything else. As a result, he never remarried.

Ann is following him; however, her appetite leans more toward criminal investigation. Like her father, who made a name for himself by being one of the investigators in the financial political loan scandal, she has helped solve some high-profile crimes.

Ann and Hank were just finishing lunch when Hank got the call verifying that the body of the young woman was Courtney Hill.

CHAPTER 11

Two uniformed police officers, personnel, and a chaplain arrived at the home of Mark Hill in the early evening. As they exited their vehicles, they could see Mr. Hill peering at them from a window.

Jill and David had stopped by Courtney's house after the party, looking for Courtney. She hadn't answered her phone and hadn't left with them in one of the last water taxis. When they didn't find her at home, they assumed she was either staying with Stephen on board or had gone off with someone else. Courtney was known to just take off on her own, from time to time. Although Jill was secretly worried that something may have happened to Courtney, she didn't share that with David, as he thinks she always overreacts to situations.

Courtney's name had become well known due to the last Stephen Knoll film. The press junket had been hard at work with press releases and interviews. Courtney appeared on the cover of several media magazines as the new, upcoming star. When Courtney didn't show up the day after the party, Mark reported she was missing. It was true that she did go off sometimes on her own, but he knew she would have called him, as she had many, many times in the past.

Mark had been worried about his daughter's newfound stardom and popularity. Even though she was a sensible young woman, he knew the dangers and pitfalls of being part of the acting business. He went through some of those pitfalls with his ex-wife, Holly. Holly, at one time, was an upcoming star. She made the turn into pornography upon being promised the moon and the stars by a man she was having an affair with, which ended Mark and Holly's marriage.

When Mark saw the uniformed police pulling up in front of

his home, fear gripped him. He opened the door and watched as the police and two others walked towards him. They all met on the stoop in front of his open door.

"Are you Mark Hill?

"Yes, did you find my daughter?"

"May we come in?"

"Of course. What's wrong? Did you find Courtney? Is she okay?" All Mark's words just came out in one long breath.

"I'm Deputy Hargrave, this is deputy Edwards and Chaplain Reed. We are very sorry to inform you that the body we found has been identified as your daughter."

All Mark heard was 'the body' and 'daughter'. Tears slowly started streaming down his face.

"I knew it. I knew it. I knew something would happen to her being part of that parasitic world of film stars." More tears came. "She wanted it so badly and was so excited about being in a Stephen Knoll film." More tears turned into sobs. "I...I was happy for her because she was happy."

Mark rambled on for several more minutes, as the officers and chaplain listened patiently, until the tears became waterfalls, and his body began to convulse into sobs.

"Mr. Hill, is there someone we can call for you? Someone who can come and be with you?"

Mark didn't seem to hear what the officer said. He was shaking so much from his sobbing, all he could manage to say was, "Does her mother know?"

"Yes, our officers are with her now." With that, Mark's cell phone rang. When Mark answered his phone all he heard was a woman sobbing. Finally, the woman on the other end of the line spoke.

"Mark, it's Holly. Did you hear about our baby? She's gone. She's gone." Then the sobs started up again. He couldn't manage to bring forth any words and just held the phone out to one of the officers. The officer took the phone and said, "Ms. Hill, would you please give the phone to one of the deputies?"

The officer at Holly Hill's house was trying to console her as well.

Finally, when Mark got some control of his emotions, he was asked if he was up to going with them to the coroner's office to identify the body. He was told that his ex-wife would be meeting them there. He nodded, got his coat, and was escorted to the car.

Mark Hill met his ex-wife, Holly, at the coroner's office to identify Courtney. He was much more emotional than his ex-wife. He could hardly control himself. At first, shock, then denial. He didn't believe that the body he was looking at was his daughter's. He was brought back to reality when he heard Holly confirming that the body was Courtney. He just couldn't accept that Courtney was lying in front of him.

He raised Courtney practically by himself. She lived with him after the divorce, all through drama school, and even when she started to get bit parts. Courtney, in some ways, was his best friend. He felt sick and hollow inside, and alone.

Holly stared at her daughter's body, and flashes of her as a small child filled her mind. Happier times for sure. That is when she and Mark were making a life together. Things were good for a while, then she got bored with homemaker stuff. When she went back to her previous life, things started falling apart for her and Mark. Feelings of guilt filled her mind. Tears streamed down her face as she left the coroner's office.

CHAPTER 12

Ann met Hank at the home of Stephen Knoll. She parked her car behind his, in front of the house. It was a modest ranch style home set back on a corner lot, with a huge fountain in the middle of the manicured lawn.

"Good morning. How's the Empress running these days?"

"Hi there. She's running pretty well. Thanks for asking. I'm so glad Dad kept Mom's car. Every time I slip behind the steering wheel, I feel she is with me."

"Who knows, she probably is," Hank replied.

Ann smiled and said,"Okay Cowboy, let's do this."

Ann and Hank walked together up the Lannon flagstone steps. Hank used the door knocker to announce their presence. The door opened and a tall, well-built man motioned for them to come in.

"You must be Detective Johnson. I'm Stephen Knoll. Please come in."

"Thank you. This is Ann Hart, the investigator on this case. Again, thank you for agreeing to meet with us this morning."

"Absolutely."

"We are here about Courtney Hill."

"I have been hearing about how she was found on the news all morning. Terrible, terrible, terrible. A tragedy. She was in my latest film and to think that she is now dead, is hard to believe. She was at my party. Beautiful young woman. Such a tragedy."

"Yes, it is. What we know is what you are hearing. Do you have a list of people that were at your party?"

"I think my manager can put together a fairly good list. We had people coming and going all evening. Everyone was supposed to sign our guest book when they came aboard. There are always those people who won't. However, we do have the list of people who were invited and can check the responses as well."

"That's good. When do you think we can have that list?"

"Bob Kerry, my manager, is on his way over now. He called me the minute he heard the news about Courtney. He probably has everything with him. He never goes anywhere without taking half of his office with him. You are welcome to wait."

"Thank you. Do you mind answering a few questions while we wait?"

"No, anything I can do to help."

"Were you and Courtney Hill personally very close?"

"Over time, we got to understand each other and did become close."

"How long have you known her?"

"I met Courtney shortly before I started shooting my last film. Hany Al Shariff saw Courtney rehearsing for a bit part in another movie. He was impressed and introduced her to me. After meeting Courtney, Hany, who was the financial backer for the film, convinced me to hire her for my upcoming movie. We actually wrote a part for her, and I must say, none of us were disappointed."

"Tell us more about your relationship with her."

"Really, not much more to tell you. She was easy to direct; she always came prepared, and that gave her the star quality of a professional. Most of our conversations were centered around the industry."

The conversation was interrupted by the sound of the knocker. Without waiting for someone to answer, the door opened and in walked Bob Kerry, Stephen's manager. He was carrying a well-packed briefcase, which he immediately plopped down on a nearby chair.

Stephen introduced Detective Johnson and Ann Hart and informed him why they were there. As it turned out, Bob did have several lists with him. He was going to have his clerk combine them when he got to the office. Detective Johnson assured Bob that he could work from the lists, since they were a combination of the invitations, responses, and the guest book from the people who boarded the boat.

"Mr. Kerry, before we leave, do you mind answering a few

questions for us?"

"No, of course not. Ask away."

"What was the nature of your relationship with Courtney Hill?"

"I didn't really have a relationship with her. I manage Stephen's affairs from the office. If I happened to go to the set, I would see her there, of course. 'Hi, have a good day, or bye,' was the extent of our conversations. It is a terrible thing. Do you know what happened to her?"

"As we told Mr. Knoll, we know just about as much as you guys are hearing on the news."

"Did either of you ever see her with a boyfriend or anyone she might have been dating?"

Both Stephen and Bob shook their heads, indicating no. However, Stephen said, "I've seen a man hanging around the set when Courtney was filming. She didn't seem to know him. I also saw him several times outside the studio when we were all leaving."

"Mr. Knoll, Mr. Kerry, thank you for your time. We will get these back to you as soon as possible. Mr. Knoll, also, we would like to search your yacht."

Stephen responded quickly, "It isn't my yacht. We rented it from a friend who keeps it at the rental place down on the Marina. The name of the boat is B-Yacht'ch."

"Thanks, I'm sure we won't have any trouble finding it with a name like that."

"Well, thanks again." With that, Stephen showed Ann and Hank to the door and said, "Anytime."

As they walked down the steps, Hank said, "I bet some guy named that yacht after his ex-wife." Ann laughed and agreed. They each walked to their respective cars, still chuckling.

Ann followed him to the station. While the clerk was making copies of the lists, they discussed what they learned from Stephen Knoll and Bob Kerry. They were querying the validity of their answers, wondering who the man was that may have been stalking Courtney. A clerk interrupted their brainstorming with copies of the lists.

"Well, let's go talk to Mark Hill. Come on, Red. Afterwards, if you have the time, we can check out that yacht."

"I have nothing but time. You know how I get when following a story."

"Like a dog with a bone."

"You are right! Although, I'm not sure I want to be compared to a dog. Seriously, thanks again for including me in this investigation."

"I wouldn't have it any other way," Hank responded.

CHAPTER 13

Hank and Ann drove together to Mark Hill's home in Westwood Village, a small section in the western side of Los Angeles. Approximately 50,000 people live in the village and it's adjacent to the city of Beverly Hills. Mark Hill's home is a Spanish style stucco in the older section of the village. Detective Johnson had called to make sure Mr. Hill was up to talking. He knew he and Mrs. Hill had a rough emotional time at the coroner's office. Mr. Hill said he was grateful for the call and said he was up to talking to the detective.

Mark Hill saw the car pull up and was anxiously waiting for them outside by the door. He shook Hank's hand, as well as Ann's, and escorted both of them into a Saltillo tiled foyer. They followed him to the living room, and he gestured for them to sit down. Ann chose a straight-back chair to the right of Mr. Hill, and Hank sat on an ottoman to his left.

"As you know, I am Detective Hank Johnson, the one who called you. This is Ann Hart, my investigator. We would like to ask you some questions about your daughter. Are you up to it right now?"

"Yes, Detective, I know you must do your job. I'm as good as I can possibly be right now. What do you want to know?"

"Again, I am sorry for your loss. Did your daughter have a boyfriend or someone she saw regularly?"

"No, not that I'm aware of. She did have a boyfriend about a year ago. However, they stopped seeing each other for some reason or another. They had not been seeing each other all that long, a couple of months or so. Courtney and I were close. I'm sure if she were dating someone else, she would have told me. She mostly hung out with her two best friends, Jill and Lisa."

"Would that be Jill Huffer and Lisa Crane?"

"Yes."

Hank continued to ask questions about Courtney's habits and schedules. While they were talking, Ann, after getting permission from Mark, went to explore Courtney's room. The room had a light, airy feel to it. An old-fashioned shade had been pulled up, allowing the sunlight to come through the lacy curtain. The room was surprisingly sparse for a young woman. Especially for a young woman who recently became a film star. Black, grey, and white were the primary colors, with some red here and there. Ann did notice some dried red roses on the dresser. They were laying on a small satin pillow. The card next to them said, "*You are a star.*" The inside of the card had six stars with one word in each star, "*Where do we go from here?*"

While Ann was holding the card, Hank wandered into the room.

"What do you have there?"

"It's a card from someone she may have been seeing. Let's ask Mr. Hill if his daughter spent nights away often. Her closet doesn't have as many clothes as I would think she would have, being in the industry that she is in. Also, her dresser isn't full."

"Maybe she was a minimalist."

"You know what I think? I think she was seeing someone on the sly. Maybe even staying with them from time to time. Did the guys who picked up her laptop find anything that could give us some insight?"

"No, not as far as I know. The laptop had her financials, social media platforms, and emails. None of the emails popped up as red flags. They are still going through her laptop. Too bad we don't have her phone. It probably went with her into the ocean. We need to get on the yacht that Stephen rented."

Before they left, they asked Mr. Hill if Courtney spent nights away from home. He told them that she sometimes spent the night at either Lisa's or Jill's. He didn't know anything about the dried roses or the card.

"Thank you, Mr. Hill, for letting us come and talk with you about your daughter. Again, we are sorry about your loss."

Mark held out his hand to both Hank and Ann and said,

"Thank you both for caring."

While Ann was walking toward her car, Hank called out suggesting they go back to the station and ride together to check out the yacht. She nodded and got into the Empress.

As Ann drove away from the curb, she thought back to the card she had pulled from her Tarot deck this morning. It was the Seven of Swords, which indicated deception or something hidden. She thought about that for a moment and decided to let the day continue to unfold before jumping to conclusions. However, it did look like Courtney had been hiding something. Yet, on the other hand, it could be Stephen Knoll or his manager, Bob Kerry, or even Mark Hill for that matter. *Time will tell*, she thought.

CHAPTER 14

Ann and Hank wove through the maze of parked boats to get to the rental office. They were greeted by a middle-aged man in his fifties, with sandy blonde hair and a tanned weather-beaten face. He looked like he had lived on the beach his entire life.

"How can I help you folks?"

"I'm Detective Hank Johnson and this is Ms. Ann Hart, an investigator on a case we are working. We are here to look around the yacht that Stephen Knoll rented a couple of weekends ago. The name of the yacht is B-Yacht'ch."

"Does it have something to do with that movie star who was found by a fishing boat?"

"Yes, she happened to be on the yacht for Mr. Knoll's party."

"I bet you're looking for clues, right?"

"Right. Can we see the yacht?"

"Sorry, of course. I am sure the owner wouldn't mind. It's docked right over there. It has been thoroughly cleaned, but you're welcome to check the boat out. Let me get the keys."

He came back with a whole ring of keys, the kind you might see hooked on a custodian's belt.

"It's too bad about that young woman. Do you think she was murdered?"

"We really can't talk about the case, sorry."

"No, I'm sorry. I shouldn't be prying. It's that we just don't get a lot of excitement around here. The last excitement around here was when one of our resident's dogs fell off their houseboat into the water. A sand shark spotted the poor thing and was going for it when someone from the dock threw a large object at the shark. I think it was a metal can of some sort. That startled it, and the shark turned away. Someone in a dingy scoped up the dog."

"That certainly sounds like it was quite the commotion. Is the yacht much further?"

"No. Just on the other side of the gate."

Mr. Sandy Blonde Hair led the way down the ramp toward a locked gate. He thumbed through the ring and pulled out a key that fit the lock, and the gate opened. With the set of keys in his hand, he led them down another walkway to the yacht. After climbing up the stairs in the rear of the boat he unlocked the sliding paneled door at the top to the interior.

"Here are the keys, just lock up when you guys are through."

Hank nodded, took the huge ring of keys, and set them down on the steps. Then he and Ann started to look around. The yacht was pristine. It looked like it was not only cleaned, but it appeared that all the wood had been polished. The impressive upper deck had a small, curved bar on each side, with sofas that ran down the center of the deck. It looked more like a beach clubhouse than a boat. Ann flipped on a switch, and lights appeared behind each bar and on the bottom of each sofa. They looked at each other as if to say, "So this is how the rich live."

After searching the entire upper deck, they went down to the main floor. A long, mirrored, bar ran half the length of the deck, with chrome and leather bar stools making the bar area shine like a million crystals in the sunlight. Covered tables and chairs were scattered throughout. They checked the bar area, lifted table and chair coverings, and found nothing. Not even a speck of dirt.

Feeling a bit defeated, they went back to the stern where they boarded the yacht. Climbing down the staircase, they realized there was a duplicate staircase on the other side of the flat deck. A shelf-like deck in between the two staircases housed a small, motorized inflatable boat and a set of jet skis. Two small ladders led up to that small deck.

"Well, we have gone over everything and have found nothing."

"True, yet there is something. If she were thrown off this yacht, it would be from here. It's the most logical place."

"You're right. However, not much down here to look

through."

"I'm going to check those covered chaise lounges."

Ann did just that. Her intuition was uncanny. If there was something to find, she surely would find it. She uncovered the first lounge chair and realized it was bolted down. So, she crawled under the chaise lounge chair and started to feel between the metal rods and the fabric that were under the seat. Nothing. She then uncovered the second chaise lounge chair and started to do the same thing. Her actions were interrupted by her spotting a tiny spot on the deck floor near the bottom of the chair.

"Hey Cowboy, come over here. I am hoping I found something."

Smiling, Detective Hank Johnson walked over to where she was kneeling and said, "What is it, Red?"

"Look at this. Could this be a speck of blood?"

"Don't know. It could be. I have a testing kit in the car. Let me go get it."

While Detective Johnson was gone, Ann marked the spot and continued to look around. She finished crawling around under the second and third lounges and found nothing. She then went to the shelf like deck, climbed up the couple of steps to where the boat and ski jets were housed, and started to look around. She really didn't know what she was looking for. In the beginning, she thought she might find Courtney's cell phone. Now, she was just looking to look.

While she was looking through the little boat, Detective Johnson returned with the test kit. He bent down, covered himself with his jacket, sprayed the luminol substance on the tiny speck. and it lit up.

"Yep, it's blood, all right. I swear Red, if there is something to be found, you will find it."

Ann smiled and then said, "I was rummaging through the little rubber inflatable boat and found this toolbox. It was sitting strangely on its side, like someone was in a hurry to put it back. When I opened it, all the tools were neatly snapped into their appropriate slots, except for one slot which was empty. It just seems odd to me. Everything else in this toolbox, in fact everything on this yacht, is neat and organized. What do you think?"

"I think you might be on to something. The coroner said that she had a small stab or puncture wound. Hmm, a tool? Could be that this empty slot may have housed our weapon?"

"She could have been with someone on this deck who stabbed her, then fell into the water, or was pushed. The killer could have been anyone who was at the party."

"Or the killer could have been on the water already, came alongside the back of this yacht, berthed his or her boat, climbed aboard, and killed her."

"Yes, it's feasible. Well, we have our work cut out for us. There were a lot of people at the party, so let's go over the list."

They locked up, returned the ring of keys to Mr. Sandy Blonde Hair, and inquired about the toolbox. He confirmed that all the tools should have been in the box. It may not have been checked when it was recently cleaned, but the toolbox had been checked before the last rental, which was by Stephen Knoll.

Hank ordered a forensic team to scour the yacht for any more telltale signs of blood. He then met Ann back at the station to go over the party list and decided who they were going to interview next. Holly Hill was the next logical person to be interviewed. Maybe she knew of someone who Courtney may have been seeing. It was decided. They would interview Holly Hill next. It was late in the day, but when Hank called Holly with the intention of planning a time for the next day, she asked if they could make it this evening instead.

"Red, we're on if it's not too late for you," Hank said.

"I'm good, as long as we can grab a hot dog on the way," Ann retorted.

"No problem. I'll even buy."

CHAPTER 15

Holly Hill lived in the Southeastern part of the San Fernando Valley known as Burbank. It's close to where she works, since it is surrounded by several film studios. Her home was in one of the few gated communities nestled close to the hills. After entering the code to open the gate that Holly provided for Hank, he drove through several winding streets until he and Ann came upon Holly Hill's house.

It was a modern, one-story with impeccable landscaping. Beautiful rose bushes lined the front of the house, bordering a manicured lawn. Simple and elegant looking. Like her ex-husband, Mark, she was waiting outside by the door. Hank and Ann walked up the walkway to the door and were greeted half-way by a pretty woman who appeared to be in her early forties, although, she would probably admit to mid-thirties. They were invited in and offered something to drink. Ann and Hank declined.

"Thank you for taking the time to talk with us. I'm Detective Hank Johnson, the one who called you, and this is Ann Hart, my investigator. We are working on finding out what happened to your daughter."

"Thank you. I appreciate that. How can I help?"

"Well, first of all, we are sorry for your loss."

"Thank you. These past days have been surreal. Even though Courtney and I didn't spend a lot of time together, I knew she was always there."

"Ms. Hill, do you know if your daughter was dating anyone?"

"No, not that I am aware. She was seeing someone a year ago. I think that just fizzled out. Although, I heard that he popped back up in her life just a couple of months ago. I don't think it was any more than getting together for a cup of coffee."

"Do you know his name?"

"Not sure. Something like, Donny, Danny, Davon. Oh, I really don't remember. You may want to talk to Lisa or Jill. They are her two best friends. Even though I'm Courtney's mom, we weren't that close. She didn't approve of my chosen career. I don't blame her. I know that her father was worried she would fall into the same trap I did and get involved with the wrong people. Sometimes, in the film business, promises and offers are made that are hard to pass up."

Hank and Ann took turns asking questions hoping the answers would lead them to who killed Courtney. Holly really didn't have anything more than what they already knew. They decided to leave and follow up on the ex-boyfriend.

"Thank you for talking with us. We may need to come back with some follow-up questions."

"You are welcome. Of course, come or call anytime. I want to help in any way I can. I wasn't a very good mother, maybe I can make it up to her now in some way. Just let me know what I can do to help."

Detective Hank Johnson acknowledged and thanked her again. He and Ann bid their goodbyes and left the gated community.

The conversation in the car primarily revolved around this ex-boyfriend of Courtney's. They decided they needed to talk to her friends, starting with Jill.

As Ann drove home, she thought again about the tarot card she pulled that morning that indicated deception or something hidden. She felt sure that Holly Hill wasn't hiding anything. She was pretty forthcoming about her career, her failed marriage, and her relationship with Courtney. That left Bob Kerry and Stephen Knoll.

It was a long day for Ann. When she got home, she filled the tub, poured herself a glass of wine, and eased herself into the water. Soaking in the hot water, sipping her wine, she just wanted to relax and not think. Her mind had other ideas and kept going back to the investigation. Ann finally gave up, got out of the tub, swallowed the last bit of wine, and just collapsed into bed.

CHAPTER 16

Mark Hill's depression over his daughter's death is causing him to just wander aimlessly around his house, not really knowing what to do with himself. He's not eating or sleeping. He wants to cry, but the tears just won't come. He hasn't been to the office in days. Today, he decided to push himself, at least, to have something to eat.

It was all he could do to get two pieces of bread and smear mayonnaise on them. In rote fashion, he put turkey and cheese between the two slices, deciding to forgo the lettuce and tomato. That just seemed like too much work to him. He grabbed the bag of chips and sat down at the table, without his plate. His mind was so befuddled that he left his food on the counter. As he was getting up to reach for his sandwich, the doorbell rang. He grabbed the plate, put it on the table and left the kitchen to answer the door.

"Oh, Craig, come in."

Mark Hill had hired Craig Reed to follow and watch over his daughter. He was worried about her with all the media attention. He forgot about Craig, until now.

"Mark, I am so sorry about Courtney. I followed her to the studio, to the store, even to the yacht party."

"Well, what happened Craig?"

"I don't know. I got into the same water taxi with Courtney and her friends. I watched her mingle. She was flirting, talking, and enjoying herself. Then suddenly, she wasn't around anymore, and I couldn't find her. I assumed she noticed me, gave me the slip, and took a taxi back to the dock. I stayed until I saw her friends leaving and left at the same time."

"Please come sit down with me. I would like the company. Just made a sandwich. Would you like one?"

"No, thank you. I'll just have something to drink. Mark, I'm sorry again about Courtney."

Mark and Craig continued to talk and speculate about Courtney's demise. Craig told Mark that he did see Courtney talking to a young man outside the studio one evening. It seemed to me that he had waited for her to come out to talk with her. She knew him, because they hugged each other when they met. That was the only time I saw him.

"Thanks Craig. I know you did your best to watch her. She has always been a feisty girl and pushed the envelope every chance she got. I just wonder what she got herself into this time, or if it was because of her new fame. Her face was all over the newsstands, on magazine covers, and industry papers. The detectives who are looking into what happened to Courtney were here asking if she was seeing anyone. I told them I was not aware of anyone. Maybe she was seeing the man you saw her with. Oh, I don't know. I just don't know."

Mark continued to talk about Courtney and Craig just listened. As he talked, tears started to come slowly at first, then more until he was sobbing. Craig didn't really know Courtney, yet witnessing Mark's sobbing brought a few tears to his own cheeks until he was crying with Mark. The men just sat at the kitchen table with a half-eaten turkey and cheese sandwich and untouched chips, crying like babies.

When Mark stopped sobbing, he wiped his face and nose with the napkin sitting next to the half-eaten sandwich and said, "I'm so sorry. I haven't been able to just let go and let it all out. My grief and sadness have been too overwhelming to do so. Until now, I guess, I just needed a friend to talk to and cry with. Thank you for being here with me. Craig, I miss her so much."

CHAPTER 17

Jill Huffer and David Weisberg were having their morning coffee when Hank and Ann knocked on the door. David answered the door and was taken back for a moment, because they were just expecting a young woman. After introducing themselves, David invited them in to join him and Jill for coffee. Hank and Ann did join them at the table but declined the coffee.

"Jill, thank you for agreeing to meet with us. I am Detective Johnson, and Ann Hart is the investigator on this case. We are sorry for your loss. I understand that you were one of Courtney's friends?"

"Yes, I was one of her best friends."

"Again, I am sorry," Ann said.

"I can't believe she is gone. We were just together at a yacht party. David was with us as well. "

"Jill, may we ask you some questions about the party?"

"Yes, of course."

"Who did Courtney spend most of her time with at the party?"

"She was with Lisa Crane and I when we first got to the party. Then she went off on her own to talk to several of the people who were in the film with her. There were a lot of people wanting her attention, so she walked around and talked to people she knew and introduced herself to people she didn't. She would pop back by Lisa and me occasionally."

"Did she spend any time with any one particular man?"

"Not really. She did spend some time with Stephen Knoll and his investor, Hany Al Shariff, then moved on."

"Do you know of anyone who would have wanted to hurt Courtney?"

"No. I don't know her new acquaintances or friends. Since

she starred in Stephen Holler's film, Lisa and I haven't seen as much of her as we used to. Although, I can't imagine anyone wanting to hurt her." Jill started to break down. Her voice cracking, and tears starting to come down her face, she continued, "Courtney was kind and a very loyal friend."

Ann grabbed the tissue that was on a nearby table and handed it to Jill. Then asked her, "Was Courtney dating anyone."

"Not that I know of. She was seeing someone about a year ago, but that ended. Courtney got bored with their relationship."

Ann continued, "Do you remember his name?"

"Yes, Dan. However, I don't think I ever knew his last name."

"Thanks. Did Courtney sleep overnight here sometimes?"

After wiping the tears from her face, Jill answered, "No not really. Lisa, Courtney, and I would have girl nights from time to time, and most of the time they both went home. Only if we drank a lot would they stay, and that wasn't very often."

Hank turned to David and asked, "Were you very close to Courtney?"

"Well, yes and no. Yes, because she was Jill's friend, but no, not personally."

Hank and Ann once again gave their condolences and said their goodbyes.

"Hank, did you notice how David rolled his eyes when Jill said that Courtney was kind?"

"Yes, I wonder what that was about. He looked like he wanted to say something but changed his mind.

Ann didn't mention the tarot card she had pulled out that morning. The card, once again, indicated something hidden. Two days in a row, she had pulled the same card. She felt sure that David was hiding something. She thought to herself, *what did he want to tell us, what is he hiding, who else is hiding something?* Ann knew that she would talk with David again, alone.

Hank and Ann continued talking all through lunch about

the case and they were anxious to talk to Lisa Crane.

CHAPTER 18

David just about choked when Jill described Courtney as kind. He would have used different words to describe her. Words like, mean, thoughtless and selfish.

"Jill, are you all, right?"

"Yes, thank you David. Being questioned by the police just brought the realness to Courtney's death. I was just not ready to accept that she's gone. I don't know if I will ever be ready to accept it. I loved her so much."

"I wonder who killed her." You know, she could be a mean person at times. I just wonder if she ruffled someone's feathers the wrong way."

"David! Courtney was not mean, a little terse at times, but not mean. How can you say that?"

"Well, I think Lisa would disagree with you. Courtney flaunted her success in Lisa's face. She knew that Lisa wanted to act and hasn't had the breaks that she had. I think that is mean, and maybe a bit self-centered as well."

Jill disagreed with David, poured more coffee for herself, sat back down, and asked David to leave. She was feeling overwhelmed with grief and now her boyfriend is bad mouthing her friend who was just murdered. It was too much for her.

David loved Jill so very much and didn't want to lose her. He left wishing he hadn't said anything about Courtney, knowing that it had upset Jill. He was still shaken up by Courtney threatening to blackmail him.

At the yacht party, Courtney confronted him with his secret and threatened to tell Jill. He never found out what his ultimatum would have been. After he told her she should mind her own business, they were interrupted by one of Courtney's newfound fans.

Just thinking about that conversation infuriated him once again. Courtney never got to finish her conversation with him. *Well, I don't have to worry about that anymore. My ultimatum died with her.*

CHAPTER 19

"I understand that Detective Johnson and his investigator sidekick are interviewing everyone who was on Stephen's yacht party. I am concerned that something will bring them back to us."

"Stan, stop worrying. They are looking for who murdered Courtney, not who's skimming money from Stephen's books."

"I know you're right. Yet, if Courtney found out, anyone who is doing any snooping of any sort can find out."

"She only suspected something was up."

Stan Ritkowski and Bob Kerry had been skimming money for months from the profits of the last four films that Stephen Knoll produced. It started very innocently. One fine day when Stan was doing a reconciliation of the accounts, he found a mistake he had made months before. A mistake that showed considerably more cash in the bank than what was shown in the books.

He figured since he made the mistake, and no one had noticed, he would just leave it alone and transfer the money from the account into a new account under an assumed name. Bob got involved when Stan got lit one night and let it slip. Since then, Bob has been making deals, adding a higher percentage to the financial package with the studios, and Stan moves the extra money into the account under the assumed name of Kenneth Sheets.

In the meantime, Ann started to do her own online research. *I know there is more to Courtney than just being a newfound star and as Jill put it, kind*. She found the ex-boyfriend from some of the posts and pictures that popped up on her social platform. Ann thought to herself, *hmm, Dan Rose. Well, Mr. Rose, let's check you out.* She found several Dan Rose's online. However, there was only one that lived in California. Ann believed it was a pretty good bet that he was the one dating Courtney. *If he was the one who gave her the card that was found in her bedroom, and she ended the relationship, he might have flipped out and killed her. Anger, that definitely could be a motive. Let's just see what he has to say for himself.*

Ann continued searching the web for other links to Courtney. When she was satisfied, she decided to pay Dan Rose a visit, on her own.

CHAPTER 20

Ann pulled up in front of Dan Rose's apartment in Santa Monica, a coastal city west of downtown Los Angeles. She parked the Empress in the underground parking garage of the building. She hadn't wasted time trying to find a spot on the street because that was next to impossible these days. Walking towards the sign indicating the direction of the lobby, her mind wandered to the days she was looking for a place of her own and even wondered if she hadn't been in this garage before.

Ann lives in a condominium in one of the new security buildings built a couple of years ago. She calls it her sanctuary and loves spending time just sitting and watching the sunset over the water. Ann had been one of the lucky people who got a front unit overlooking the ocean.

She always loved the view of the ocean, yet she didn't like being in the water or lying in the sun. Once she tried to sunbathe and that didn't turn out well. Ann's sunburn required a trip to the emergency room and that was the extent of her sunbathing.

Ann looked for Dan Rose's name on the resident list in the lobby. When she found it, she pushed the appropriate code that would alert him that there was someone in the lobby. A voice came out from a little box on the wall asking who it was. She told the box her name and why she was there. To her surprise there was an immediate response from a buzzer sound by the door. She grabbed the handle quickly, for fear it would stop before she could open the door. When she walked through the door, she saw a man standing at the end of the hallway. It was Dan Rose waiting for her.

Dan had been expecting someone to come question him ever since he heard the news about Courtney. He was surprised it took so long.

Ann approached Dan and said, "Hello, I am Ann Hart, an

investigator working on the Courtney Hill murder case. Are you Mr. Rose?"

Dan nodded his head yes, and said, "I was expecting someone to show up."

"May I ask you some questions?"

"Of course, please come in."

Daniel showed Ann into his apartment and offered her a seat. Ann took a seat and asked if she could record their conversation. Again, he nodded his head indicating that it was okay. Ann began, wanting to know what his relationship had been with Courtney. He validated what she had learned from Courtney's mom and her friend Jill.

They did go out for a while, and even though he felt things were good, Courtney didn't feel the same way. She told him that she was bored and needed more excitement in her life.

"I have to admit, I was angry and became bitter. Then I saw her in that movie and read all about her newfound fame and realized that it was the life she needed to live. She did reach out and invited me to the celebration on the yacht."

"Did you go?"

"No, that lifestyle isn't for me. I thanked her and declined."

"Why do you think she reached out and invited you to the party if you guys had ended your relationship?"

"Well, a couple of months ago, we met for coffee and sort of rekindled our relationship."

"What do you mean, sort of rekindled your relationship?"

"We started seeing each other again. However, Courtney didn't want anyone to know. Actually, I thought she was seeing someone else at the same time as seeing me."

"What gave you that idea?"

"She wasn't always available, or she would make a date with me, then cancel it. I did confront her about it, and she told me I was just being ridiculous. In any case, our relationship, if you could call it that, fizzled out and once again, she dumped me."

"When was the last time you saw or talked with Courtney?"

"When she called to invite me to Stephen Knoll's

celebration party."

Ann thanked Dan for his time and was getting ready to leave, but then she remembered the card that was in Courtney's room. She stopped, turned around and asked, "Did you ever give Ann a romantic card at any time?"

"No, not really. I only gave her a birthday card and that was in the beginning of our relationship, so it wasn't romantic."

Ann thanked Dan and left his apartment.

After Ann left, Dan grabbed his lightweight jacket and keys and jetted out the door for a jog on the beach. He decided to walk a few blocks to the ocean to clear his head. Once at the ocean front, he jogged slowly down to where the water meets the sand and picked up his pace until he was almost at a full run.

Suddenly, he thought he heard his name. Then he heard it again. "Hey Dan, Dan Rose."

He looked toward the shoreline, and he saw a man waving his hand. The man motioned for Dan to come towards him. As Dan started jogging toward him, he recognized the man as his friend Jim.

"Hey Jim, what's up?"

"Nothing much. I just thought I'd come down to the beach for a hot dog. Can I buy you one?"

"Sure, why not."

Jim turned to the vendor and said, "Two hot dogs with everything." They grabbed their dogs and sat down on one of the picnic benches near the edge of the sand.

"How did the other night go?"

"What night?"

"You know, when you went to see your ex-girlfriend."

Jim was the guy Dan borrowed a boat from to cruise over to the yacht party. He wasn't going to join in the festivities, he just wanted to see Courtney. Dan had something special he wanted to talk to her about. When she called to invite him, he did tell her "No" for the party. However, she agreed to meet him on the lower deck. His plan was to meet her on the lower deck, take her out on the boat and discuss something with her. He wanted to ask her a question.

As Dan told Ann Hart, he and Courtney had rekindled their relationship a couple of months before. She called him one night to come over, and he did. They continued from that night forward. However, she didn't want anyone to know that they were together again. He loved her so much and was so proud of her newfound stardom. He understood her wanting privacy due to all the media press she had received due to starring in Stephen's film. But he wanted more of her than she seemed willing to give. Courtney felt pressured and ended their rekindled relationship.

"Not very well."

"Why, what happened?"

"Nothing, that's what happened."

"What do you mean, nothing happened? Didn't you talk to her about, you know?"

"Yes and no. As I was approaching the yacht, I saw someone standing with her. I knew Courtney didn't want anyone to know she was meeting me. So, I waited and cruised around for a while until I saw the person go back up the stairs to the next deck. When the coast was clear, so to speak, I pulled up alongside the rear of the yacht and asked Courtney to climb in and go with me for a quick ride. She agreed. As it turned out, that was the only thing she agreed on that night."

Dan took the last bite of his hot dog, gulped down the rest of his drink and continued telling Jim how their ride went.

"Courtney was playing me. When I started talking about why she dumped me once again, and that maybe she would reconsider, she started laughing. I just sat there navigating the boat here and there kind of in a stupor. When I got myself together, I asked her what was going on, why she was laughing. She told me plainly that I was just someone to play with from time to time. I never bothered telling her that I really wanted a future with her."

Just then a group of skaters rolled by interrupting Dan's story. At that point, he decided to stop because he was sounding too much like a whiney girl. He just ended with, "After being humiliated, I took her back to the party and dropped her off."

"Sorry man. I know you really loved her."

"Thanks. Yes, I did."

Dan decided to end the conversation, thanked Jim again and continued down the beach. As he jogged along the shoreline, his thoughts went back to that night. He pictured Courtney laughing at him and felt the humiliation all over again.

CHAPTER 21

Ann was lost in her thoughts about Courtney Hill as she drove away from Dan Rose's apartment. *He wasn't telling me everything.* She wondered what Courtney was really like, who killed her and why. During the conversation with herself, she caught sight of a Ferris Wheel and realized she was driving past the Santa Monica pier. Watching people on the boardwalk, memories replaced her thoughts and the one-sided conversation. Ann remembered walking on the pier with her mom, eating cotton candy. Sometimes they would stop for ice cream and walk all the way to the end holding hands. She lifted her right hand and patted the dashboard of the Empress and said, "Thanks mom."

As she drove on, her boardwalk memories faded and once again her mind went to Courtney Hill and then to Dan Rose. She pulled out her phone and dialed Hank's cell phone. He picked up on the first ring.

"Hi Red, what's up?"

"I just left Courtney's ex-boyfriend's apartment. According to him, the last time he heard from Courtney was when she invited him to the yacht party, which he declined. She did break up with him last year. However, they got back together for a brief time just over a few months ago."

"Did you believe him?"

"Well, he sounded convincing, but I have a gut feeling that he wasn't telling the whole truth. I had thoughts since he and Courtney had gotten back together, that he wrote the card to her, but I don't think so. According to Dan, he thinks she might have been seeing someone else as well."

"Hmm. Well, your gut feelings are pretty reliable, so maybe we will have to circle back around and talk to this Dan guy again. Today, I'm on my way to Lisa Crane's. Do you want to meet me there?"

"For sure. Send me the address, and I will see you there."

Ann went back to the conversation in her head. *Who would have a motive to kill Courtney? Dan Rose would, since she didn't want to continue their rekindled relationship. Stephen Knoll wouldn't kill his new cash cow. Oh, how I hate that expression. His accountant or manager wouldn't have a reason, or at least we don't know of one. Maybe through more conversation, this might change.*

Once again, her one-sided conversation was interrupted. This time by Hank who was waving her towards a parking place. She parked, took the keys and as she was about to open the door, Hank beat her to it.

"Hey Cowboy, thanks. Chivalry isn't dead after all." They both laughed.

"Come on Red, let's go find out what Lisa can tell us."

Lisa opened the door wearing green sweats which complemented her light reddish hair and her fair skin.

"Are you Detective Johnson?"

"Yes, and this is Ann Hart, my investigator. May we come in?"

"Of course." She motioned for them to take a seat pointing towards a room that had several chairs and a love seat. Lisa sat down on the love seat, Ann, and Hank each took a chair.

"Thanks for agreeing to see us. We would like to ask you some questions about Courtney Hill. Her father told us that you were one of her best friends."

"Yes, I was."

"Was she seeing anyone?"

"No, no one that I was aware of. She was seeing a guy named Dan for a while last year. Courtney told Jill and I that she ended that because she was bored. He didn't stimulate her enough. I guess she got more stimulation from Stephen Knoll."

"What do you mean? Was she seeing Stephen Knoll?"

"I don't know. She eluded that she had an 'in' with him. When we were planning what we were all going to wear to the party she mentioned that Stephen wouldn't mind if she brought Jill and I because she had an 'in' with him. Jill and I suspected that maybe she was secretly seeing him."

While Lisa was talking, Ann was taking notes in her notebook. She realized that in her notes from their interview with Jill, that was never mentioned. Questions, she had more questions.

Ann asked, "How long had you and Courtney been friends?"

"Ever since Drama School. We clicked right away. She was more of a go-getter than me. Whenever a talent scout was scheduled to come, she made herself available for more conversation than any of us other girls. She was much more aggressive than the rest of us. It worked for she was chosen more often for small parts in independent films."

Ann continued to dig into Lisa's feelings about Courtney's success, "How did you and the rest of the girls feel about Courtney being selected more often for parts?"

"We were fine with it, for all of us got small parts from time to time."

Hank jumped into the conversation. "So, you think that Courtney was seeing Stephen Knoll?"

She was seeing someone and when she made that remark about having an "in" with Stephen, that kind of gave it away. Yet, when we asked her about that later, she denied it. So, not sure who she was seeing."

"Jill didn't mention Stephen or that she thought Courtney was seeing anyone. What makes you think she was seeing someone."

"Just knowing Courtney so well. She was kind of giddy from time to time and she wasn't the giddy type. She only got that way when she was seeing someone she liked, and she hadn't been that way since Dan."

"Who did she spend most of her time with at the party?"

"Courtney spent some time with Jill and me in the beginning of the party. She mingled with all her newfound friends. She spent some time with a lady named Francine and a couple of times I saw her with Hany Al Shariff. At one point I saw her go down to the lower deck in the back of the yacht. Didn't see her come back up since Jill and I started to walk around the yacht exploring the downstairs. When we came back to where the action was, I didn't see Courtney. Actually, I never saw her again."

Hank continued, "Did Courtney have any enemies or someone who would want to hurt her?"

"No, I don't think so. Everyone really liked her. She may have ruffled some feathers when trying out for parts, but not enough for someone wanting to hurt or kill her."

"Miss Crane, thank you for your time. We may be back with more questions as we continue our investigation."

"Anytime."

Hank and Ann left. Ann's mind started to chatter. *There were inconsistencies between her story and Jill's, small ones, but in a murder investigation small details matter.*

They walked over to Ann's car. Hank leaned on the car and asked, "Lunch?"

"Sure, you buying?"

"I thought it was your turn," Hank said, laughing.

"But first, bear with me. I want to check something out. She pulled out her worn tarot deck from her bag. He knew it was a ritual that she had for many years. Sometimes it helped her see things more clearly or differently, and sometimes it was just being curious.

She shuffled a couple of times, then blindly pulled out a card. The Moon. Ann stared at it for a bit, collecting her thoughts.

"That one mean anything?" Hank asked.

"Deception. Hidden truths. What we know might not be the whole picture."

"Sounds about right. Lisa's story had holes. Either she is holding back, or Jill is. Maybe both. Let's go eat."

Ann slid the card back into the tarot deck and put the deck back into her bag, then climbed into the Empress.

They each drove off in their respective cars, meeting up at one of their favorite hamburger spots for lunch. Upon arrival, they were escorted to 'their' table, and each ordered a hamburger and a beer.

While they were waiting for their hamburgers, they drank their beer and went over Ann's notes from all their interviews. The

Moon card was still lingering in the back of Ann's mind when the burgers arrived. They stopped going over the case and just enjoyed each other's company.

CHAPTER 22

"Hany, what am I going to do?" Stephen Knoll and Hany Al Shariff were having lunch in a small out-of-the-way restaurant near the marina. Stephen wanted to talk with Hany without being recognized. Due to all the publicity about Courtney Hills' murder, he had become more of a celebrity than he was before. It had become so bad that there was always at least one reporter stationed in front of his house.

"Stephen, what do you mean? Is it about the reporters?"

"No. Although, these reporters have become a problem. I'm talking about our plans for the next movie. Now that Courtney is dead, what do we do?"

"Well, I'm still your investor, and I'm not pulling out. Your films are blockbusters. I know that Courtney was a big draw. However, you had good films before Courtney. You groomed her, why not another girl. Groom another newcomer."

"Oh, I don't know. To be honest, it's not just about the film. A girl got murdered at a party that I hosted. A young woman who had her whole life ahead of her, just as she was starting to make it in the film industry. In a way, I feel responsible."

"Although, I do understand why you may feel that way, let me assure you that you are not responsible for her death. Courtney had secrets."

"Hany, we all have secrets."

"I know. Some of us have more secrets than others. I think that Courtney was in the category of 'more.'"

"What do you mean, more?"

"She had two close friends, Lisa Crane, and Jill Huffer. Neither one of them knew if she was seeing someone. When I talked with her at the party, she led me to believe she was involved with someone romantically."

"How did that conversation come about?"

"To be honest with you, I wanted to date her and did try several times. She shut me down each time. Courtney was very flirtatious with the crew on the sets, as well as with other actors in our production. I thought she was anybody's girl, but the conversation we had at the party changed my mind on that."

"Did you find out who she was seeing?"

"No, I didn't, and she didn't say. For someone who was involved with someone, she certainly didn't act like it on the yacht. She flirted with every man there, whether they were a guest or part of the hired staff. She was an enigma, for sure."

"I must be deaf, dumb, and blind, for I wasn't aware of any of these things. I didn't even know you were interested in her. So, you and Courtney never did get together?"

"When I first met her, we flirted a bit. After she started working with you, she stopped and went into rejection mode. I got it. She had a plethora of men always around her, especially toward the end of production. I guess she hooked up with one of them. We will never know."

"It didn't seem like Detective Johnson, nor his investigator Ann Hart, knew if Courtney was seeing someone. When they interviewed me, that was one of the questions they asked. Hany, have they talked with you yet?"

"Not yet. I know they interviewed Bob and Stan, but they haven't gotten around to me yet. Not sure I can add anything to their investigation."

Hany continued to reassure Stephen about their upcoming film projects. They finished their lunch and took a walk out along the pier. As Stephen was looking over the rail into the water, his thoughts returned to Courtney. Hany was thinking about Courtney as well, *one of her secrets got her killed.*

CHAPTER 23

"Lisa, thanks for coming over. I just can't seem to shake this depression I have been feeling ever since Courtney's death," Jill said, teary eyed.

"Of course. You know I'll come anytime. Sorry you are still feeling down. I haven't been myself either since Courtney left us."

"I feel so guilty for the way I talked to her the night of the party," Jill added.

"What do you mean?"

"You know, the way Courtney was flitting around every man on the boat like a bee around flowers. I said something to her about it. She wasn't too amicable to hear what I had to say."

"Yeah, she was acting like a queen bee at that. Stardom went to her head. What all did you say?"

"I suggested she may want to cool her flirting and stick to polite conversation. After all, she was Stephen's new star, and her behavior reflected on him."

"What was her response?"

"She gave me one of her Courtney looks and just said she was just so happy. I sensed it was more than her newfound stardom that was creating so much sparkle in her. I think she was seeing someone. You know, how giddy she gets when a new man enters her life. The last time I saw her like this was when she hooked up with Dan."

"I remember. I also have had the feeling she was seeing someone, or at least, met someone new who excited her. She usually didn't keep things from us. I wonder if she was seeing someone, why was she so secretive about it?"

"Oh, I don't know Lisa. I just know that I sure do miss her."

While Lisa and Jill were reminiscing about their times with Courtney, Detective Johnson and Ann Hart had finished their hamburgers and were already interviewing Francine Brittone.

"Thank you for making time for us today. We are trying to gather as much information as we can about what happened to Courtney Hill."

"Such a tragedy."

"Did you know her?"

"No, not really. I did talk to her at the party for a little while. She was all over the place, flitting like a butterfly. One could tell she was really on cloud nine."

"What did you and Courtney talk about?"

"Not much. She told me how Hany Al Shariff got her into Stephen's film and how exciting it had been for her to be working with all the people involved with the production. She was quite taken with all the fanfare she was getting. I got the impression that she was looking for someone at the party."

Ann jumped in before Hank had a chance to say anything and asked, "What gave you that idea?"

"As we were talking, she kept turning her head from side to side, like she was looking for someone. At first, I asked her if she was waiting for someone, but she said no, just that she was hoping someone she knew would show up."

Ann continued, "Did she happen to say who?"

"No. However, I got the feeling it was somebody special, if you know what I mean?"

Hank took back over by asking, "Special, in what way?"

"You know, special, like someone romantically in one's life."

The conversation between Francine, Hank, and Ann continued for a bit longer. When they left, Ann felt a sense of excitement because she knew she was onto a story. *Who was Courtney seeing secretly?* She was sure that someone special gave her that card.

As Hank and Ann were walking out of Francine's home, Hank said, "Red, how about having dinner with me tonight?"

"Hamburgers and beer?"

"Ha. Ha. No, a nice dinner. A real date."

"Now we've talked about that. Hamburgers and beer now

and then are one thing, but a real date? We've talked about keeping our personal relationship casual."

"Okay. We can keep the dinner date casual. Will that work?"

"Cowboy, you are relentless. Yes, dinner would be nice. Remember, casual!"

As Ann drove away, she thought, *I knew something would come up with Hank today. The cards are never wrong.* Ann had pulled the Two of Cups from the Tarot deck, which represents partnerships, mutual attraction, engagements, and relationships.

CHAPTER 24

Ann woke up the next morning raring to go. She didn't want to admit that she had a good time at dinner. She liked Hank and could see herself in a more serious kind of relationship with him. However, she didn't want the complication of what that would bring to her life. So, for now, she would continue working with him and enjoy their occasional burgers and beer.

While drinking her morning protein shake, as part of her morning ritual, Ann pulled a card from her Tarot deck. It was the Lover's card. At first, the card gave her a start. Then she realized the card wasn't about her. Right then and there, Ann knew she was right about Courtney seeing someone. She was certain that was why she pulled that card.

Once again, Ann went over her notes about the Courtney Hill case. Ann decided she was going to find out who she was seeing secretly. Jotting down some ideas as to how to go about finding out, she decided the first thing was to stop by the station and check out Courtney's laptop. She felt sure there would be some clue somewhere on her social media accounts.

Ann finished her drink, rinsed out the blender and her glass, grabbed her notes and bag, and out the door she went. She was on a mission. Once again, she started having one of the conversations in her head about the case. Then the internal dialogue went back to her dinner with Hank. She was clear that she didn't want to complicate her life with a romantic relationship with him, yet she really enjoyed their deeper conversation last night. Her mind switched back to the case.

Walking into the station, she noticed that Hank's car wasn't in the lot. She felt a twinge of disappointment. Shrugging it off, she entered the building, and once she was through the screening process, she went directly to check out Courtney's laptop. Settling in behind one of the desks, Ann started her digital journey.

Ann typed in Courtney's name, and her bio came up.

Courtney Hill was an American actor who rose to stardom due to her role as Cora Alcott in Stephen Holler's film Changes. She graduated from an arts college and started her acting career appearing in several independent films......

The article went on to talk about her family and other details of her short life. Ann continued her search by going through her media platforms. She didn't know what she was looking for but knew that she would know when something popped up. She was coming up empty and decided to check out her photos.

She was surprised by how many pictures of Courtney there were. Not only were the photos that Courtney had taken and uploaded to her accounts, but the ones that the internet had as well. Pictures of scenes from her films, group shots, award ceremonies, and a plethora of others. A couple of the group photos caught her eye, especially one.

"Deputy Huber, can you help me with some photo identifications from these photos?"

"Certainly, Ma'am."

Deputy Huber worked with Detective Johnson and was up to speed on the Courtney Hill Case. He joined this station after working two years in the jails. Huber was a sharp deputy and was assigned to the Hill case immediately. All the interview notes had been typed up by the clerks, and Deputy Huber had assembled them in neat folders for both Ann and Detective Johnson. Neither of them had ever had their interview notes typed so nicely, let alone put in folders. Huber was kind of an anomaly, but a great asset to the investigation.

"Here, let's concentrate on this guy in the back watching the group. There is Courtney with Stephen, Hany Al Shariff, and some of what looks like the film crew. Look at the guy in the background. He looks like he got in the picture by mistake. Here he is again in another group shot standing off to the side. Can we find out who he is?"

"If he is in our system. Let me see what I can find."

Deputy Huber took the laptop and connected to the

station's photo identifying computer. Ann knew about reverse imaging but had never seen this type of equipment before. A few minutes later Deputy Huber said he had a name for her.

"Derek Green is the man's name. He is the husband of Monica Green, who is the CEO and Chairwoman of IRF, International Reel Films. Isn't that the studio where Stephen Knoll produces his films?" Huber asked.

"You are right. Now that's very interesting. It shines a whole new light on this case. Thank you very much!" Ann replied.

"Yes ma'am, anytime."

"One more thing, do you have any personal information on the Greens?"

"Mr. Green owns a prop house in North Hollywood for the studios. They live in Bel Air, and according to my information, they do not have any children."

Bel Air is a ritzy residential community in the foothills of the Santa Monica Mountains. Two stately entrance gates off Sunset Boulevard led to winding streets lined with lavish mansions on large properties with lush vegetation. Popular with celebrities and the entertainment industry elite.

"Thanks again. I think I will pay Mr. Green a visit."

Ann left the station and that twinge of disappointment came back as she walked to her car. Hank's car still wasn't in the lot. She wondered where he might be. Ann thought about calling to let him know where she was going then stopped herself. Just then, her phone rang.

"Good morning, Cowboy. I was just wondering where you

were."

"Good morning, Red. Moving slower than usual this morning. On my way to the station now."

"No more late dinners for you."

Hank chuckled and replied, "I was hoping that was just the first of many."

Ann, ignoring his reply, quickly said, "I found something interesting and I'm on my way to check it out."

"Wait for me and I'll check it out with you."

Ann filled him in about the Greens and her suspicions about Mr. Green and Courtney. She told him she really had wanted to go it alone, as she could smell a story. He understood her desire to chase a story but reminded her that anything to do with the Courtney Hill investigation was his responsibility, even though she was the investigator on the case. Just then, he pulled into the lot.

Smiling and feeling happy with herself, she drove out of the lot on her way to the prop house, alone. Ann convinced Hank to let her go without him. He had agreed on the condition she promised to call him afterwards. Ann found the prop house on one of the back streets of North Hollywood.

The parking lot was lined with large pillars and columns one might find in the ruins of the Roman Coliseum. Ann found a spot near the door in front of a large sphinx statue. She sat in her car for a moment, excited about this case, yet feeling its weight. Ann took in a deep breath and let the weight of the case settle over her.

Reaching into her bag, she pulled out her tarot deck, shuffled it, and blindly pulled out a card. The Moon. Again, the Moon. Secrets. Illusions and things lurking beneath the surface, hidden truths waiting to be uncovered. Staring at the looming entrance to the prop house, she thought, *if that isn't a sign, I don't know what is*. She put the card back into the deck and stepped out of the car. If Derek Green is hiding something, she was going to find out.

She got out of her car, locked it, and kept her eye on the statue, like she was on guard just in case it came to life.

Ann walked through two large hand carved wooden doors.

Each one had a doorknob in the shape of a dragon head. She found herself standing inside a large warehouse with several aisles to choose from. She called out, "Hello." Her greeting came back to her as an echo. Ann called out once again, and once again, the only response was her echo. She decided to pick an aisle to go down, hoping to meet up with someone.

Couches in every color with chairs to match, dressers, of every shape and size, paintings from modern to traditional, lined the aisle she chose. It seemed that the aisle would never end when she came to a fork, with one aisle going one way and the other going another.

She thought, *now I know how that rat must have felt. I'm in a maze just like that rat.* A man interrupted her thoughts suddenly appearing from nowhere. "Hey, what are you doing back here? Can I help you?"

Ann was somewhat startled by this man's sudden appearance and jumped a bit. After she composed herself, she responded. "Yes, I hope so. You have quite the place here."

"I take It that you haven't been in a prop house before."

"No, my first time."

"Is there something in particular that you need?"

"Yes, there is. Are you Derek Green?"

"Yes, I'm Derek."

"My name is Ann Hart, and I am a criminal investigator working with the police on a murder case."

"A murder case? How can I help you?"

"I know that your wife is the CEO and Chairwoman for the studio that Stephen Knoll produces his films. Did you ever meet Courtney Hill, one of the stars in his last movie?"

"Yes, I did meet her. Such a tragedy."

"How well did you know Courtney?"

"Oh, not very well. Just met her a couple of times at the studio."

Ann pulled the two photos that Deputy Huber printed out for her and showed them to Derek. Is this you in these pictures?"

Derek Green looked at what Ann was holding and appeared to be surprised to see himself in the photos. "Why yes, it is.

Although, I don't remember these shots."

"Looks like you are watching the group. Or someone."

"I wasn't watching anyone. I must have walked into the room and got into the photo accidentally."

"Do you remember what you were doing or where you were going when these photos were taken?"

"No, not specifically."

"Were these pictures taken at the studio?"

"Yes. If my memory is correct, they were celebrating the success of Stephen's film."

"Do you remember if you stayed in the room when they were done with taking these pictures?"

"I really don't remember. They were always stopping and taking impromptu pictures. Not sure which time this was. Why so many questions about these photos?"

"Just part of our investigation into the murder of Courtney Hill. Do you know if Courtney was dating anyone seriously?"

"I have already told you that I just met her a couple of times and really didn't know her."

"Yes, I know. I just thought you might have heard something through the "studio grapevine.""

"No, never heard anything about her dating anyone."

"Were you at the yacht party that Stephen Knoll hosted?"

"Just briefly. My wife went alone, and I joined her a bit later."

"I didn't see your name on the list of guests that attended."

"That's probably because I took my own boat to the party. My boat is in a marina not far from where the yacht was anchored. My wife and I have a condo there, and I happened to be staying there that weekend entertaining some clients."

"Did your wife go back with you on the boat?"

"No. My clients were staying at the condo, so I left after I paid my respects and had a drink with my wife. She stayed at the party."

"Did you leave alone?"

"Of course. What are you getting at?"

"Nothing really. Just gathering information. Detective

Johnson is the lead detective in this case, so he might want to ask you more questions."

"Okay, but I really don't have much more to tell."

Ann thought, *I think you have a lot more to tell.* Ann thanked him for his time and left. As she walked back down the aisles, she looked around for an office. She had a hunch about Derek. She needed to get into his office.

CHAPTER 25

On her way back home, Ann called Hank to fill him in on her talk with Derek Green.

"How about I meet you somewhere for lunch, or dinner later."

"Thanks, but I think I'll just grab something and take it home. I have a couple of personal errands to run. Hank was disappointed; however, he knew when she made her mind up, there was no changing it. But he was willing to try.

"Okay Red. See you tomorrow."

Ann settled herself at her desk with the sandwich she picked up from a local deli. She looked through the window in front of her desk and watched the far-off waves. *I think my visit to Derek Green's warrants another card. He wasn't telling me everything he knew about Courtney.* Ann's internal dialogue was off and running about her visit with Derek Green.

Once again, she reached for her tarot deck. It had become second nature whenever she felt stuck or unsettled. She let the cards speak. Shuffling carefully, she drew a card. The Seven of Swords. Deception. Someone sneaking away with something that wasn't theirs. Lies. Secrets.

I knew it. Somehow, I must get into his office. If I could get a sample of his signature and compare it to the card we found on Courtney's dresser, I bet it matches. I could just ask him, but I don't want to let on that I suspect anything. I have a better idea.

She decided not to fill Hank in just yet and decided to act on her 'better idea'.

Late that night, she drove back to the prop house, not really expecting anyone to be there. Parking on one of the side streets, she quietly exited her car, locking it from the inside to avoid the beeping sound made by the key fob. It was past midnight, and she didn't want to attract any unwanted attention. After walking two blocks, she saw the big columns that she had parked in front of earlier in the day. Ann looked around and didn't see anyone, so she walked across the parking lot. She was just a little way from her mission. The building looked different, then realized it was because the items that were displayed outside when she was there earlier, were now, more than likely, inside.

Ann approached the door, still looking around. No sign of life. She tried the door, all the while keeping her eye on the Sphinx statue which seemed to stand guard. She laughed at herself for being intimidated by a cement statue. The door was locked. *I thought it would be.*

Ann slowly walked around the building looking for a back door. She came upon a large, corrugated metal overhead door. *This must be where the big items go in and out.* The door apparently had not closed properly since there was a small opening at the bottom *Hmm, I wonder if I can fit through that opening. I think I can if I lay flat and slide in. After all, it's not really breaking and entering, since the door is technically open. Yeah, right!*

Ann did just that. She laid down perpendicular to the opening and started scooching under the door. She didn't realize there were small stones, or gravel pieces on the ground where she was laying until she started to move. *Maybe this wasn't such a smart choice. Well, I'm committed now.*

She continued to wiggle under the door. Each time she scooched, the little stones poked at her back. It was a slow process.

"Oh, crap."

Ann slid her hand up on to her stomach and felt for blood. The bottom of the door had scraped against her. *Thank goodness it's rubber or I'd be bleeding about now. All this to find a signature.* Ann took one last scooch. She was in.

Once on the other side of the door, Ann stood up, brushed herself off and checked to see if she had any scratches or cuts on her back. None that she could feel. All was good so she decided to feel her way around. The phone's flashlight was just enough for her to see the aisle she found herself standing in. After getting her bearings she realized she was in the back of the building. *Now to find Mr. Green's office.* Ann decided to walk the outer aisle against the wall. Halfway around the inside perimeter of the building she spotted a door.

Unlocked.

What are the chances?

Ann entered, shining her light in the room and laughed. She was standing in the bathroom. *When you need one, you can't find one.* She left and continued her search along the wall. About ready to give up when Ann saw another door. Again, the door was unlocked. She walked in shining her light.

"Bingo!"

Ann had found Mr. Green's office. Now to find something with his signature.

The office was sparse with a desk, two chairs, a filing cabinet, and a printer. Ann looked all through the desk and found nothing. Searching the file cabinet didn't prove much better. The files contained printouts of the companies who rented or purchased props. Nothing handwritten.

Dad always told me to follow my hunches. It doesn't look like my hunch is paying off this time. But I still think Courtney was seeing someone and Derek might be just that someone. If I could just find something with his signature.

Finding nothing handwritten, she left the office, closing the door behind her. With the help of her phone's flashlight, Ann started back the way she came. She got halfway down the aisle when she heard a noise coming from the back of the warehouse.

The metal door was moving.

She froze. The door was going up.

Using the wall as her guide, she crept slowly toward the noise. It suddenly stopped and she assumed the door was now open. Again, she stopped and just listened. It was quiet. Ann started feeling her way once again. As far as she could tell she was halfway to the door.

Lights shone through some of the props lighting up part of the warehouse. At first Ann thought that someone had turned on lights in the back. Then she realized the light was coming from the headlights of a car or truck.

She walked a little farther down the aisle keeping herself hidden by some of the tall props. Ann decided she would wait and see what was going on and then somehow get out through that open door.

Several men walked through the door each carrying what looked like a carousel horse. *What are they doing here past midnight? I could ask myself the same thing.*

"Hey guys, hurry it up. I don't want to be here all night," one of the men said.

"Okay, okay. These horses are heavy!"

"Greens got a good thing going here."

"There's a couple more horses in the truck. Let's get them and get out of here!"

"Wait up, I have to use the john."

"Well hurry up. Like I said, I don't want to be here all night."

Ann panicked. One of the men was going to be coming down the aisle where she was hiding.

Ok Ann, think.

She started back down the aisle toward Green's office and heard footsteps. *He is much closer than I thought.*

Ann didn't think she would make it to the office in time. She didn't have her phone light on anymore and even though her eyes were adjusting to the darkness, she wasn't sure where she was. She stopped and listened. Footsteps. Right behind her.

Taking a chance, she detoured off the aisle and squeezed herself between what looked like two large pieces of furniture. Just as she brought in her leg, Ann saw the man walk by.

Whew! That was close.

She stayed hidden until the man walked past her again. Once she felt that he was far enough away, she squeezed herself free from her hiding spot. Slowly creeping back down the outer aisle toward the back door, she could hear the din of men talking. As she got closer, she could see the men through an opening to her side.

"Hope everything came out alright," one of the men teased.

"Very funny."

"Come on guys, stop with the jokes. Let's finish up."

Ann watched the men go back to the truck for the remaining horses and decided she should try to slip out the door while they are bringing them into the warehouse.

She quickly continued down the aisle and stopped about twenty feet from the door. Still in the dark, Ann felt sure that once the men came back into the warehouse, she could slip out without being noticed. She waited for her chance.

"I'll be glad to get rid of these heavy things. Come on guys, almost done," said the same man. Ann thought, *he must be the boss.*

All the men were in the warehouse now. This was her chance.

She slid against the wall until she was a couple of feet from the opening. *Just a couple of more steps and I'm out.*

Ann crept to the opening and then bolted out the door.

Whew, made it!

Suddenly, she felt someone grab her from behind.

"Where do you think you're going? She felt herself being dragged into the warehouse. "Hey guys. Look what I found."

"What the hell? Who are you?"

"I work here. Who are you?" Ann replied.

"I'm asking, not answering. So, who are you?"

"I am a part-time worker for Mr. Green. He asked me to do some filing for him. Because I have another job and two children, I couldn't do it until after they went to bed. Now what are *you* guys doing here? He didn't tell me anything about people coming tonight."

"Delivering stuff for Green. He didn't tell us about you either. Do you have a name?

"Yes, I have a name. My name is Ann, and he didn't know I was coming late, but like I said, I couldn't come any earlier. So now that we all know why we are here, I must get back home. So, we good?"

"Guys, what do you think?"

"Don't know. I don't trust her."

Ann popped in and said, "Let's call Mr. Green."

"No, it's too late. He'll skin us all alive. I say that we keep her with us until tomorrow, then we can check with Green."

"Sounds like a good idea."

Ann playing a hunch, hoping this one would work out better than the last one, chimed in the conversation and said, "that is a lousy plan. My kids are home alone, and I must get to my other job in the morning. Let's just call Mr. Green."

Secretly, she hoped they wouldn't call him.

"Enough jibber- jabber. Get her in the truck."

One of the guys grabbed Ann's arm and pulled her towards the truck. When he loosened his grip to open the door, Ann yanked her arm free and bolted across the parking lot.

The guy that let Ann get a way, pulled his cell phone out of his pocket, punched several buttons and when the caller answered, he said:

"Boss, we got a problem."

CHAPTER 26

Panting and out of breath, Ann reached the block where she parked the Empress. Her nerves were on edge. She hoped that she had not been followed, although she couldn't shake the feeling that she had been. Ann approached her car as quickly as she could. She used the key to open the door so as to not make any clicking or beeping sounds and slid in behind the steering wheel. Even though her hand was shaking, she did manage to insert the key and start the car. She looked around and didn't see anyone, so she felt safe enough to start inching the car away from the curb. With car lights off, she slowly drove down the block.

Once she was far enough away from the prop house Ann turned her car lights on and sped up. She drove home on autopilot as her thoughts were all mixed up in her head. *What the hell was I thinking? Man, there's more to this Cortney Hill case than meets the eye. What was in those carousel horses? More than likely, drugs. Did Courtney know about this? Was she romantically involved with Derek Green? Did his wife find out?*

By the time she got home, her shaking had stopped, but her mind was still swirling. Ann poured herself a glass of wine, sat down at her desk, and emptied her mind out into her notebook. When she was done, she poured herself another glass of wine, sat back down at her desk, and looked out her window at the moon's reflection shining on the ocean. She finished her second glass of wine, walked to her bedroom, and just collapsed on her bed. She was down for the count.

Ann was jolted awake by the ringing of her cell phone and saw that it was Hank. At first, she thought of not answering it, then decided it was best to talk with him. Barely awake, she answered her phone, glanced at the clock, and saw that it read 8:15 A.M.

"Good morning, Cowboy, what's up?" Ann said, trying to

sound perky and awake.

"The sun, the ceiling..."

"Ha ha. You are funny, and so early in the morning."

"I try. On the serious side, can we meet this morning? I want to go over the case with you. Say in about an hour?"

"Sure but, give me until ten. I need a little more time to pull myself together this morning."

Hank agreed. Ann took off her yesterday's clothes, and jumped into the shower. She dried herself off in record speed, pulled her black slacks up, zipped them, and then buttoned up the white blouse she chose to wear. The weather had been fickle lately, so she grabbed her black sweater, along with her briefcase, purse, and a protein drink.

The shower has to suffice for my meditation, but I do have time to pull a card, and she did. She gasped, for it was the Ten of Swords. *Today is going to be a very interesting one.*

Ann would normally take the main roads to the station, not worrying about the traffic, but because Detective Johnson's request to see her seemed more urgent than normal. She took the smaller side streets, avoiding any gridlock. She pulled into the parking lot and parked her car next to Hank's. Somehow, that made her feel close to him.

One of the detectives greeted her as she walked into the station. "Hank is in the back getting coffee."

"Thanks detective." Ann replied and walked to his desk where she plopped all her stuff down, then walked to the back. Hank saw her, got that "happy to see you" smile on his face and offered her a cup of coffee.

"No thanks, just had my protein drink. What's up? Something new in the Courtney Hill case?"

"Yeah, went by the studio yesterday to see Stephen Knoll. I wanted to see if he remembered anything else that might help our investigation. No luck. He really didn't have anything else to add to what he already told us. Stephen suggested we talk to Stan, his accountant, once again. He said that Courtney and he were pretty close friends."

"Did Stan have anything to add?"

"Unfortunately, he wasn't in his office. I did leave a message for him to give me a call. However, while I was with Stephen, I saw Lisa Crane at the studio. He told me that she had come to him asking for a part in his upcoming movie. She was there to try out for one of the parts."

"It didn't take her long to step into Courtney's footsteps."

"That's what I was thinking."

"Maybe we should do a follow-up with her as well."

"I was hoping you would do the follow-up with her. Maybe she would be more open and candid with you."

"Sure. I'll talk with her. But first I have something to tell you."

Ann started telling him about how she felt that Derek Green was not being truthful about not really knowing Courtney all that well. She believed he could be the person who wrote the card found in Courtney's bedroom. Ann went on to tell him that she drove to the prop house, and how she got in to look for his signature to compare it to the card.

Hank interrupted her. "What were you thinking? You went alone? At night? That's breaking and entering, Ann."

Ann feeling embarrassed by being chastised by Hank, she winced and replied, "I didn't think I'd get caught."

"What do you mean caught?"

Ann realized too late that she said more than she intended to. She tried to lighten the mood by telling Hank how she got into the prop house, so technically, it wasn't breaking in, it was only entering. Hank smiled to help relieve the tension between them, even though he didn't find it all that funny.

Ann felt the tension between them lessening, so she thought now was a good time to tell Hank about the guys she saw carrying in the carousel horses.

"Bringing in wooden horses at that time of the morning? That screams of drugs. Did you check them out after the men left?"

"Well, not exactly! You see, as I was sneaking out one of the men caught me and let's just say, they were very displeased by my presence. I was able to get away from them."

"You what? Got caught? Reckless, but I'm glad you got away. But if you're right this could be a motive. You just might have come up with a motive for Courtney's murder."

Ann popped in, "What if she found out that the studio's prop house is a front for drug trafficking? I'm sure Mr. Green would not have been happy about that."

"I know. That is what I have been thinking. I believe Courtney started seeing Derek secretly sometime during the filming of her movie or shortly after its release. His prop house would be the perfect place to meet. On one of their private meetings, she may have discovered his secret and threatened to expose him."

"There's one more thing I need to tell you. After one guy caught me, we all had a very charming conversation about what I was doing there. I told them that I worked for Mr. Green and was doing some filing."

"Filing in the middle of the night? Did they buy your story?"

"Yes and no. The bottom line is, I gave them my name. For some reason, I wanted Derek Green to know that I know about his secrets."

"You are playing a very risky game if he is the killer."

"I know. Sorry about the 'breaking and entering' thing."

Ann and Hank continued to discuss the case for a few more minutes, and their conversation ended with Hank asking Ann out for dinner. She said she'd meet him for a casual bite to eat to give him an update on her conversation with Lisa. He was disappointed because he wanted a bit more ambiance for dinner but was glad she said yes to something. Ann left to go talk with Lisa Crane, and Hank left to go talk with Derek Green.

CHAPTER 27

Lisa hung up with Ann Hart feeling apprehensive and immediately dialed Jill.

"Hi Lisa, how are you doing?"

"Well not sure. You know that investigator working on Courtney's case?"

"Yes, Ann Hart."

"Well, she is coming by to ask me more questions. Did she call you too?"

"No."

"It makes me nervous talking to her, or the Detective."

"Don't worry. You don't have anything to feel nervous about. They just want to find out who killed our friend. I'm sure they will be talking to everyone a second and maybe even a third time."

"Gotta go. She's already here." Lisa barely ended her call with Jill, when she heard Ann at the door.

"Good morning. Thank you for agreeing to see me."

"Of course. Come in."

Ann walked over to one of the straight back chairs and sat down. Lisa sat on the couch. Ann noticed Lisa sat down with her hands clasped together resting in her lap. When she started asking some questions about Courtney, Lisa started to wring her hands.

"Is there something wrong? You seem nervous."

"No, nothing is really wrong. I just get upset when I or anyone talks about Courtney. Life without her seems surreal. I miss her so very much. To think about the last time we were together was a celebration for the success of the film she starred in. Just isn't fair."

Ann agreed that sometimes life isn't fair. She pursued that a little further with Lisa by asking her more in-depth questions about her relationship with Courtney. Lisa did bring up the fact that when they were in drama school together, Courtney got more opportunities than the other girls. Ann pressed her on how she and the other girls felt about that. Lisa said that they all felt she got all the breaks.

Ann asked if she could think of anyone that was jealous enough to have harmed Courtney. Lisa couldn't think of anyone since everyone in the class had been a little jealous of Courtney.

"If jealousy was the motive for Courtney's death, then, we would all be guilty."

Ann found it curious that suddenly Lisa could discuss Courtney's death in such a casual way, when earlier she got upset. Ann decided to change directions. Knowing full well what the answer was, she asked Lisa if she recently had any luck with auditions. She did say she had. However, she changed the facts a bit. Lisa said that Stephen Knoll had contacted her to audition for a part in his upcoming film. Ann thought, *I wonder why she doesn't want me to know that it was the other way around, that she had contacted Stephen Knoll.*

Ann continued talking with Lisa for several more minutes before she decided it was time to wrap up her visit.

"Lisa, just one more thing. Do you think that Jill Huff would have any reason to want Courtney dead?"

"No, we are, or were, all best friends. I thought you and Detective Hank knew that after your questioning of Jill and me."

"Yes, that is what you and Jill told us. I am just trying to find out who killed your friend. Well, I think I got what I needed today. I will probably have more questions as we get deeper into our investigation."

"No problem. I am happy to help in any way I can."

Ann and Lisa said goodbye. As Ann walked to her car, she felt Lisa's eyes on her. It gave her a creepy feeling.

When she got in the car, she gave Hank a call.

"How did it go with Lisa?"

"She did open up a bit more this time. There is more to Lisa Crane than we know."

"What does that gut of yours tell you?"

"Jealousy is what comes up for me. How did it go with Derek Green?"

"I got held up at the office and I am just on my way now. How about meeting me there and we can talk to Mr. Green together?"

"Do you think that's smart since I was there last night?"

"Why not find out if he knows that, and if he does, he's got some explaining to do."

"I'm game. Meet you there."

Although she agreed to meet Hank there, she really was a bit nervous about going back. *I think I stumbled onto something big.* With that thought she wove her way through the traffic until she saw the prop house and Hank's car. She navigated her car into the lot and parked next to his.

Hank, who was already out of his car waiting, opened her door and slid into the passenger side. They discussed how they were going to talk with Mr. Green. After they came up with a plan, they exited Ann's car, walked to the front door, and entered the prop house. Mr. Green didn't seem to be around anywhere in sight, so Ann led Hank down the aisles toward where she saw the men carrying in the carousel horses. A voice from behind asked, "Can I help you?" Startled, both Ann and Hank turned around to face the voice. It wasn't Derek Green.

"Hope so." Hank quickly responded and continued, "We are here to speak to Mr. Green."

"Are you from a studio?"

"No, we are with the police." Hank introduced him and Ann. He knew this man was not Derek for he had seen a picture of him.

After talking with this man for a few minutes they came to learn that Derek was at a meeting at Stephen Knoll's studio and would be back sometime later that afternoon. While Hank and the man were talking, Ann wandered over to where she saw the men put the horses.

Seeing Ann walking away, the man started edging his way toward her. Hank followed. When they caught up to where she was, Ann was rubbing her hand across the carousel horse like she was petting it.

Seeing the man walking toward her, Ann spoke up, "I was here yesterday, and didn't see these carousel horses. They are beautiful. Can you tell me something about them?"

"Nope. Don't know anything about them. Wasn't here when they came in. You'll have to talk to Derek about them."

"Thanks for your time. We'll be back this afternoon to talk with Mr. Green."

When they got outside Ann told Hank that she had seen some white powder like substance on the floor underneath one of the horses and showed him a picture of both on her phone. I took the picture before you and that man, whose name I never got, showed up. Hank told her that his name was Ken Downs. He told Hank his name when Ann wandered off down the aisle.

"So, what do we have here? Drug trafficking?"

"We won't know until we search those horses, and the entire prop house. To do that we need a search warrant, and I don't have a good reason for the judge."

"How about saying that we are in the middle of a murder investigation and believe there may be some evidence in the prop house that would help in solving the case. You could always throw in that you believe that the victim was having an affair with the owner."

"It's not quite that easy, Red."

"Well, I could always pull another midnight caper."
"Really? Your last one didn't go so well, did it? Let's wait and see what this afternoon's conversation with Mr. Green brings to the table. Speaking about table, let's go grab some lunch."

Ann agreed to have a bite to eat after she promised Hank she wouldn't do anymore midnight capers. Of course, her fingers were crossed.

Hank and Ann went over the facts they had about the Courtney Hill case. They knew Courtney was killed during the yacht party. Since blood was found on the lower deck of the stern, she was either killed on the boat and thrown overboard, or someone took her off the boat, possibly still alive, killed her and threw her body into the ocean.

They knew, besides having a contusion on the back of her head, Courtney was stabbed with a sharp object that pierced the base of her skull. There was a tool missing from a tool kit found on the yacht in the shape of what could be the murder weapon.

They went over the list of the people they interviewed.

"When we talked with Stephen Knoll, he seemed genuinely shocked and upset. I know in your 'police work' everyone is a suspect. I don't think Stephen Knoll killed Courtney. She brought him a box office hit, and great financial rewards. Besides, he has a reputation of being a nice guy."

"Red, so far I agree. Then there is his accountant Stan Ritkowski and his manager, Bob Kerry. Not sure about them. The last time I was at the studio talking with Stephen, they were both there. I just chatted with them briefly, but they both seemed a bit nervous."

"Maybe they were intimidated by the famed Detective Hank Johnson."

"Maybe, but I hardly think so. It was like they were being caught with their hands in the cookie jar. Yet, my conversation with them was about the party and if they remembered anything more that might be helpful. That shouldn't have intimidated them."

"Maybe their hands have been in the cookie jar."

"What cookie jar? What are you talking about?"

"Just think a moment. Why else would they be nervous around you? One, or both, may have something to hide. From what I have read, Stephen made a considerable sum of money from last three films. The one that Courtney was in, brought in the largest revenue."

"We are investigating a murder, not hand in the cookie jar stuff."

"Okay, I'll let that go, for now. There might be a story in it for me down the road. Now to get back to the people in Courtney's world. We spoke to Jill Huff and her boyfriend David. I spoke to Lisa Crane a second time and I do have some more questions in my mind about her. Now, there's Derek Green who I think was having an affair with Courtney and now there's possibly drugs involved in this whole thing."

"We don't know if there are really drugs. White powder looking substance on the floor of a prop house really doesn't prove anything." Hank said.

"That may be true, however, why were those men delivering

carousel horses in the middle of the night if something shady wasn't going on?"

"Yeah, you have a point, but there may be another explanation, one that doesn't include drugs. Maybe we will get some answers when we talk to Green this afternoon. Let's continue to go over our list of characters. David Wesberg, Jill's boyfriend, didn't seem to hold the same warm and fuzzy feelings about Courtney as Jill. We might want to find out why."

"I agree. The same thing with Lisa Crane. She started speaking freely about how she and other girls were jealous of Courtney. Then there's Holly, Courtney's mom who is in the porn world. Who knows, maybe she was jealous of Courtney as well."

"Jealousy is certainly a proven driving force for murder. My office has checked out the rest of the people who were on the guest list and there was no one really connected to Courtney. Mostly Hollywood and film people who were there to support Stephen."

"What about Francine Brittone? She usually knows everything that goes on in the film industry. You know, who is seeing who, the next upcoming star, who's on the verge of bankruptcy or who could have killed Courtney."

"She really didn't have much to say that was of any importance when we talked with her."

"That is true. But now that some time has passed, I would like to revisit her and see if she knew, or since heard, anything about Green and Courtney."

"Good idea."

They continued talking about who could be suspects while finishing up their lunch. Hank loved Ann's enthusiasm and commitment to the case. She not only had the tenacity to follow up, but she also had heart. He had worked with good investigative reporters in Albuquerque, but they were missing heart. He just wished she was more openhearted with him.

On the way back to the prop house, Hank got an urgent call. He hit his lights and took off. Ann followed.

CHAPTER 28

Ann pulled up next to Hank's car shortly after he arrived at the scene where a body was found. He called her on the way and told her that someone had found a body in an alley not far from Derek Green's prop house. Ann found Hank talking to the coroner after weaving herself through the sea of uniformed police.

"What's going on?"

"The rubbish truck driver found the body when he drove into the alley for the trash."

"Was there any identification on the body?"

"Yes, and you won't believe who it is."

With that, Hank took Ann by the elbow and escorted her to where the body was now lying. He uncovered the man's face, and when Ann saw it, she gasped. It was Derek Green.

"Whoa! What is happening here? We need to go back to the prop house and check out those horses."

"Yep. That is exactly what I was thinking."

Before they left the scene, Hank asked the coroner if he could tell how he died. It appeared that he was stabbed in the back with some sort of sharp instrument. Ann flashed back to the tarot card she had pulled in the morning, the Ten of Swords. It represents feeling like you've been stabbed in the back, metaphorically. Ann thought, *I think Derek would disagree with the metaphorical part*. Hank determined that if Green died because of drug deals gone bad, it sure was a sloppy hit.

Earlier that day, Derek Green received a phone call from someone who wanted to meet with him. At first, he declined, but the caller was very insistent and started threatening to go to the police about using his business as a front for drug trafficking. Green agreed to meet at a coffee shop near the prop house. As he was leaving, he received another call from his manager informing him of

Detective Johnson's visit.

Ann and Hank decided to go back to the prop house to see what Ken Downs had to say. When they walked in, Mr. Downs greeted them.

"Mr. Green hasn't come in yet. I did call him to let him know you were here and that you would be coming back. He said he would be here later this afternoon. But he hasn't shown up yet."

"Ken, you mentioned that you help out 'now and then'. How often is 'now and then'?"

"I don't have regular hours. I manage his business mostly from home. I come in a couple of hours a week to discuss business with him. On the occasions that Mr. Green has to go to the studio for something, I will cover for him."

"Have you left the building since we spoke this morning?"

"No, I haven't. Why?"

"His body was found not too far from here. It appears he met with foul play."

Ken gasped and clearly was genuinely surprised. He asked if his wife knew and was told that officers were sent to her home. Hank and Ann continued asking questions and found out that Derek had quite the thing for young upcoming actors. Ann asked if Derek was seeing anyone specific. Downs said he didn't know, but that he had seen a couple of young women meet with Derek over the last few months. One sounded like Courtney. The description of the other women could be one of a hundred girls.

Hank and Ann walked toward the carousel horses and asked Ken to follow them. Ann pointed to the white powder on the floor.

"Do you know anything about these horses?"

"Mr. Green just told me that someone requested them for a shoot at one of the studios."

"Do I have your permission to look inside this horse?" Detective Johnson asked.

"Yes, of course. I don't have any objections. With Mr. Green dead, I don't see how it matters."

The carousel horse was tipped upside down, and on the underside was a small square cut. When Hank pushed on it, the small door covering the cut slid open. Hank reached his hand inside and pulled out a bag of white powder.

Ken gasped, "Is that cocaine?"

"Or heroin," answered Hank.

CHAPTER 29

Hank had Ken lock up the prop house until a team of drug investigators came to check out the other carousel horses. Several drug enforcement officers showed up, and after several hours, all the carousels had been searched. Over thirty bags of that white powder were found, packed up, and taken by the drug enforcement agents.

Ken just stood in awe, watching all the activity. He had no idea that Derek Green had a drug trafficking thing going on. Ken was told that the prop house was going to be closed for a couple of days so the agents could finish doing their investigation. He understood and left. Hank and Ann left, reconvening at the station.

Upon hearing the news of her husband's death, Monica sat down and put her hands to her head. She sat for several minutes, holding her head, not saying a word. She knew something was going on with Derek. He hadn't been himself lately.

Derek and Monica had been together for over 25 years. They met at a film festival, and it was love at first sight. They were both new to the business. Within a brief time, they both found their chosen paths in the industry.

After Derek hurt his back in a skiing accident and could no longer do the strenuous work of a stunt double, he purchased a property house in North Hollywood that was closing. Monica worked her way through the trenches of a studio, until she pulled a coup and became Chairwoman and CEO of the IRF Studio. Currently, she is the only woman CEO and Chair of a Hollywood studio.

When she took her hands away from her head and stood up, there were signs of tear stains on her face. It was clear she knew how to compose herself in stressful situations because that is what she did. Composed, she queried the deputies on the details of her husband's death.

Meanwhile, Hank and Ann were going over their notes at the station when Ann popped up and said, "I think I'd like to talk to our friend David again. This time alone. It just seemed that David had something to tell us, and he withheld it in front of Jill."

"I agree. In the meantime, I know the deputies are escorting Ms. Green to the coroner's office to identify her husband. Boy, what a mess. I want to give her some time before we talk with her."

"I wonder if she knew her husband was a philanderer."

"Well, we will find out soon enough. It would be helpful if we knew for sure if he was seeing Courtney."

"After I speak with David, I will arrange to meet Mr. Downs with some pictures of Courtney."

"Hope you're planning to see him during the day," Hank said with a little chuckle.

It took Ann a second to catch on to what he was implying. When she did, she replied with a fake laugh, "Ha, ha, ha." She was still ha-haing as she walked out of the station door. Ann didn't like to admit to herself that she liked Hank's playful teasing.

David walked into the coffee shop, feeling anxious. He didn't know why Ann Hart wanted to meet. He saw Ann in a booth near the back and walked slowly toward her. Ann stood up, greeted David, and thanked him for coming. He nodded and slid into the seat across from her.

Ann told David that they were revisiting most everyone that had been interviewed about Courtney. He assured her that he had nothing else to share that would be helpful to the case. Ann disagreed.

"David, when Detective Johnson and I were talking with you and Jill, you made it obvious that you disagreed with Jill's description of Courtney. I would really like to know your opinion now that it is just you and me."

"Not sure what you mean."

"David, come on. You rolled your eyes when Jill was telling us about Courtney. What doesn't Jill know?"

David squirmed a bit, then did a lot of ums before he started talking. Once he did, words started to flow like lava from a volcano.

"I've known Courtney ever since Jill and I met in law school. Jill and Courtney were very close, like sisters. I liked Courtney all right, mainly because of Jill. Sometimes she had an edge about her, and it showed up mostly with Lisa. There was some sort of rivalry between them. Jill could never see that. She had blinders when it came to Courtney.

Well, anyway, at one point, I ran out of money for law school. I was already up to my eyeballs in debt and couldn't get any more loans. I happened to mention it to Courtney one time when we were waiting for Jill and Lisa to get back from a shopping spree. Courtney gave me a lead as to where I could earn some quick money."

"Did you follow up on that lead?"

"Yes, unfortunately I did. When we were on the yacht at Stephen Knoll's party, she threatened to tell Jill what I did."

"Why do you suppose she would do that, since she gave you the lead in the first place?"

"Just being a bitch, I suppose. I never did find out the ultimatum."

"What did you do that you didn't want Jill to know?"

"I guess you'll find out eventually. The lead was a gig in a porno film. Holly Hill, as you know, is a porn star. She got me a part in one of the films. You know, the older woman and the young college guy."

"Yeah, I think I get the picture."

"That's not all of it. It paid well, and it got me out of debt. However, I still needed money for the following year's tuition. I agreed to another gig. Before I realized it, I was in a scene with Courtney's mom, Holly. Courtney found out and that really upset her, to say the least. That is why she was threatening to tell Jill, to get back at me for having sex with her mom."

"So, you had an argument with her and killed her?"

"No, of course not."

"I don't know, sounds like a good motive. You stood to lose your future wife and your career as a lawyer."

"I didn't kill Courtney. That's why I didn't want to tell you that Courtney threatened me. I knew once I did, you'd think I killed her."

"You had a rather good reason. Detective Johnson is going to want to talk to you."

"Does Jill have to find out?"

"Not unless you killed Courtney."

CHAPTER 30

"Hello, this is Francine Brittone, is Detective Hank Johnson there?"

"No, ma'am, can I take a message, or can someone else help you?"

"Is his investigator, Ms. Hart, there?"

"Yes, she is. I'll see if she can take your call."

Ann had just walked into the station when Francine's call came in.

"Ms. Hart, a Francine Brittone is on the phone. She wanted to talk with Hank, and since he isn't here, she asked for you. Do you want to take the call?"

"Yes, of course. Can I use Hank's desk?"

"I'll put the call through."

"Hello, this is Ann Hart."

"Thank you for taking my call. I remembered something at the yacht party that may be helpful to you and Detective Johnson."

Francine went on to tell Ann that she saw Courtney stop and talk to two men at the party and it seemed that they were disagreeing about something. She didn't remember that until recently. She happened to be speaking with one of the cast members when she remembered that she saw Courtney talking with Stephen Knoll's accountant and manager.

"Thank you, Ms. Brittone, for the information."

"You are welcome. When I think back, it did seem sort of odd. All night Courtney flitted around talking to everyone, yet never really stopped to talk to anyone in length, except those two men."

"Again, thank you for the information. I will let Detective Johnson know. If you think of anything else, let us know."

When Ann hung up the phone, she saw Hank walk into the room.

THE DECK NEVER LIES

"Hey Red, taking over my desk, I see. I must say, it suits you."

"Thanks, but I think I'll let you keep it. Just got a call from Francine Brittone. She remembered something that could be helpful."

Ann filled him in on the phone conversation.

"If Courtney and Stephen Knoll's accountant had a disagreement, it had to be about money. It's getting late and I'm starving. How about finishing this conversation over dinner?"

"Hamburgers and beer?"

"I had something else in mind, maybe dinner with a little more ambiance, like bar-b-que with our beer." Hank said with that chuckle he does when he is teasing.

"Okay, bar-b-que it is. Can't wait to see you with a red mustache." Ann retorted.

"Back at ya, and it'll match your hair." Still smiling, he continued, "Get in, I'll drive."

Hank was happy Ann accepted his invitation. He knew if he had pushed for something more than he suggested, she probably would have declined.

They did continue their discussion about Ann's conversation with Francine and Hank's interview with David. Then Ann shared her surprise about Ken Downs regarding the pictures she showed him.

"Mr. Downs confirmed my suspicion about Courtney seeing Derek Green. He also named another girl in one of the pictures I showed him. Guess who it was?"

"By the tone in your voice, I'd say it was Lisa Crane."

"And you'd be right."

"I think we need to have a meeting with Mrs. Green."

"What about talking to Lisa again?"

"No, not yet. Let her think that her secret is safe now that Derek is dead. But I think I'd like you to circle back and talk to Stan Ritkowski and Bob Kerry. They may be more receptive to talking with you than to the police."

"Got it. I will set it up for tomorrow morning. When do you want to talk with Mrs. Green?"

"Tomorrow afternoon. Call me when you are finished with the boys."

Hank poured himself another beer, sat back, and said, "Most cases there aren't enough suspects to talk about. This one, there is a plethora of suspects who could have killed Courtney. There is Lisa, who was jealous of Courtney and has risen to the top of the list. David, who was threatened by Courtney. Derek, even though he met with an untimely death. His wife, who may have found out about his cheating ways and then there is Dan, the old boyfriend."

After swallowing the last of her beer, Ann suggested that they call it a night. Hank agreed. Although, he was always hoping for a much longer evening.

CHAPTER 31

"Bob did that investigator call you this morning?" Stan asked.

"Yes. She wanted to meet at your office." Bob replied.

"What are we going to do? She must know something, or she wouldn't want to see us."

"Nothing. We are going to talk with her and see what she knows."

Bob ended the call, grabbed his jacket, and walked out the door. On his drive over to Stan's office, he was sorry that he ever got himself involved with Stan's embezzlement caper. He thought, *for all I know he killed Courtney, or had her killed. I wouldn't put it past him.*

Bob walked into Stan's office and witnessed a very anxiety ridden accountant. Stan was pacing around the room wringing his hands and had beads of perspiration on his forehead ready to drip down his face.

"Stan, get it together. She will be here any minute. Sit down, have some water and for gods' sake, stop wringing your hands."

"Okay, okay, just so worried, that's all."

Just then, the door opened and in walked Ann. Bob was a little startled and hoped she hadn't heard his concern.

Ann thanked them for taking the time to talk with her once again.

"Detective Johnson and I are still investigating the murder of Courtney Hill and had a few more questions for you."

"Please come in and have a seat." Bob continued, "Not sure what more I can add."

Stan didn't say anything. He sat at his desk drinking water, as Bob had suggested.

"You both were seen having some sort of disagreement with Courtney at the yacht party. We would like to know what you can remember about your conversation with her that night."

Bob spoke up first and said, "I really don't remember any conversation with Courtney other than congratulating her."

Stan added, "We were also thanking her for helping to make Stephen's film a success."

"What was the disagreement about?" Ann asked.

"I don't remember any disagreement, do you Stan?"

"No, I don't. As far as I can remember, we were all just having a good time."

Ann didn't believe them. She knew they weren't telling the truth. The card that she pulled during her morning ritual was the Seven of Swords. This is the card of theft or someone getting away with something. It is about being sneaky and probably the card most associated with any sort of criminal activity. When it shows up, someone is up to no good. Ann thought, *I think they have their hands* in *that proverbial cookie jar.* She didn't have much choice but to thank them for their time and leave.

Ann took the elevator down to the first floor and called Hank as promised. She left him a short message asking him to return her call.

As soon as Ann shut the door, Stan stood up and was about to say something. Bob put his finger in front of his mouth indicating not to say anything. He walked to the door, opened it, and saw that the elevator was going down. He shut the door and said,

"Well, that didn't go so bad?"

"Do you think she believed us?" Stan asked.

"I don't know." Bob answered.

"So, what do we do now?"

"Nothing, just let things alone." Bob responded, then added, "I need to get back to Stephen. We are in the middle of a major project. Talk to you later."

After Bob left, Stan sat down and thought about the conversation that just occurred with Ann and Bob. *She didn't believe us, I know it. She needs to be stopped from poking around.*

Ann's phone rang; it was Hank returning her call.

"Good morning, just finished my time with the boys."

"How'd it go?"

"Easy, because they were lying. They both got amnesia since the party and didn't remember any disagreement or argument with Courtney."

"I'd like you to keep following up with them. In the meantime, meet me at the station. We have an appointment with Monica Green."

On the way over to Mrs. Green's, Hank informed Ann that he had been assigned to help another detective with a case in addition to Courtney's.

"I won't have as much time to devote to this case for a while. Sorry, and just as things were getting interesting."

"I'll continue investigating on my own and fill you in between the cases." Ann said feeling a bit disappointed that they weren't going to be working together.

"That's not a bad idea. In fact, that's what I was hoping you'd say. Deputy Huber can help you out. I'll put him on alert. Check in with me and keep me posted, and most importantly, don't be pulling any more midnight capers."

Just then, they pulled into the circular driveway in front of the Green residence. The house was an all-white, two-story U-shape with four huge columns in the front. The columns looked as if they were holding up a circular overhang. It turned out to be a roof-top balcony. Hanging bougainvillea draped down from the balcony like Rapunzel's hair beckoning one to climb up.

"I never get used to how the other half live. It just seems such a waste for one family to live in such a huge place, when there are so many homeless people living on the street," Ann remarked.

"That's capitalism at its finest," Hank responded.

They were surprised that Mrs. Green greeted them when the door opened. The house lent itself to having a butler.

"Good afternoon. Please come in."

Mrs. Green was an attractive woman who appeared to be in her mid to late fifties, with blondish hair mixed with red highlights. She stood five foot six and weighed approximately 180 pounds, overweight but carried it well. Mrs. Green escorted them to a room off the foyer that she called the sunroom.

Hank and Ann each took a chair. Ann spoke first, "Mrs. Green, I am so sorry for your loss."

"Thank you. Please call me Monica."

Hank spoke next, "Mrs. Green…

"Monica, please."

"Ok, Monica, thanks for seeing us. Do you know of anyone who would want to hurt your husband?"

"Oh no. He was a good man. Everyone really liked him. When he got hurt in the skiing accident and couldn't work as a stunt man anymore, everyone from the studio helped him get started in the prop house. Other studios supported him using his props. He became known as the guy to go to in the business. So, no, I don't know of anyone who would want to harm him."

"I'm sorry to ask this, but how was your marriage?" Hank asked.

"If you mean, did we get along? Yes, we did. We understood each other."

"Would you explain?" Ann asked.

"We married a little more than 25 years ago. Love at first sight. We were both starting out in the film industry and had stardust in our eyes. At first it was wonderful. As time went on and Derek got more jobs and met more people, things started to change. I never knew what was going on until one day someone saw him in a compromising situation with one of the young and upcoming stars of the studio. That person thought it was their civic duty to tell me. In that case, I would have been better off not knowing because from that day on, things between us were never the same."

"Sorry. Did Derek have a habit of seeing other women?"

"Yes, unfortunately young women were his weakness. It was usually a young girl trying to get into the business or looking to land that special part. Each one would think sleeping with my husband would get them where they wanted to go since his wife is the head of the studio. What they didn't know is, Derek had no pull, with me or anyone else. When they found out, they moved on to someone else."

"Did you ever confront your husband about this?"

"Oh yes. Many times. It hurt, but I loved him."

"Would you happen to know if Courtney Hill was one of the young women he might have been seeing?"

"Not sure. Whoever he was seeing I think he fell in love. His hormones were all over the place. I don't know, he seemed happier and more excited about life and became emotionally distant from me. Something was very different this time."

"Did you ever think about leaving him?"

"Not really, until lately"

"What changed your mind?"

"Even though he had his philandering ways, we still had a good thing going. The emotional disconnection was becoming too much for me. There were other things as well."

"What do you mean?"

"He seemed worried about something."

At this point in the conversation, Monica started to break down. Through tears she asked if they could tell her anymore about how he died. Hank just confirmed what she already knew. They talked about the yacht party and Monica didn't add any more information than they already knew. When Hank and Ann were just about to leave, Ann asked Mrs. Green if she would be able to recognize her husband's handwriting, and she shook her head yes.

Ann reached in her purse and pulled out a clear bag that contained the card she found in Courtney's room. Ann handed it to Monica. When Monica looked at the card she really broke down. Crying, tears streaming down her face, Monica shook her head yes and handed the bag back to Ann. Thanking Monica Green for her time, Ann and Hank left.

After leaving the Green residence, Hank said, "Well, Red, what do you think?"

"I think, what a mess. It appears that Derek fell in love with Courtney and could have killed her if she dumped him. After all, he took his own boat to the party and would have access to the tool that I think killed her. Or, Mrs. Green could have found out about her husband and Courtney and killed her."

Hank replied. "She could be the one who stabbed her

husband in the back. She certainly had the motive. She could have killed both."

"You could be right. Couldn't tell if she was genuinely grief stricken or a hell of an actor," Ann said.

"Well, she is in the business of acting."

"What a cast of characters!"

CHAPTER 32

Ann sipped her wine and took out the notes from the case. Some things were bothering her. One of the first things, since it was fresh in her mind, was Monica Green's display of tears. Ann wasn't convinced that she was overwhelmed with the grief she displayed. It just seemed too much, phony. She thought, *why? Is she hiding something? If so, what?*

Ann jotted down some ideas around that premise. A second glass of wine seemed in order for the work at hand. Ann continued to revisit Deputy Huber's neatly typed and organized notes. Separating them in piles, she took them one by one and went over each interview with a fine-tooth comb. Ann wasn't sure what she was looking for, but she knew whatever it was, would show itself.

There it was! Derek Green said that he had taken his own boat to the yacht party because he had been entertaining clients at a condo he had in the marina. *We slipped up,* Ann thought. That piece of information was forgotten when talking with Monica. *It looks like Monica and I will be having another talk. I wonder if she will do a command performance. Can't wait to get inside that condo.*

While Ann was spending her evening sipping her wine and reviewing her notes, Monica Green was drinking her bourbon and wringing her hands. She was worried about what she had gotten herself into.

Ann was up before her alarm. Mornings were her favorite time of the day. She loved doing her meditation on the balcony as the golden sun rays shone through the clouds onto the ocean as dawn brought the light of a new day.

Ann nestled into her round wicker cushioned chair, closed her eyes, and listened to the silence around her. When she finished, she came back inside to make her protein drink consisting of almond milk, strawberries, blueberries, spinach, kale, chia seed and protein powder. As she was enjoying her morning drink, she pulled a card from her tarot deck, as she usually did.

It was the Moon. The Moon card shows a full moon with a crescent within, twin pillars, two wolves howling, a stream that runs to the ocean, and a crayfish emerging out of the water. It is a card of illusion and deception, and often suggests a time when something is not as it appears to be. Perhaps a misunderstanding or a truth that cannot be admitted.

Ann said out loud, "Well, it is going to be an interesting day."

Ann finished getting ready, left and drove the Empress down the boulevard. She dialed the number that Monica had given her and was surprised when Monica herself answered.

"Good morning"

"Good morning, Mrs. Green. Do you have a few minutes to talk?"

"Yes, what is it?"

"Your husband told Detective Johnson and me that he had taken his own boat to join you at the yacht party, since he had been entertaining clients in a condo he had in the marina. I was wondering if you would mind me checking it out."

"No, I don't mind. I can have Mason meet you with a key. Is there something in particular you are looking for?"

"Not really. But you never know what little things can help with an investigation. I can come by and get the key if that is easier for you."

"Mason is running some errands for me today. We are putting things together for the memorial service. He is out now. I'll call him and have him meet you there, say in about an hour?"

"Wonderful. Thank you. I know this is a trying time for you. Again, I am so sorry for your loss."

Ann arrived at the address that Monica had texted just a little after Mason. He recognized her and stopped walking. Ann waved, found a place to park the Empress, and walked over to Mason.

"Thanks for meeting me here."

"Yes, Mrs. Green asked me to give you the key to Mr. Green's condo."

"Oh, I didn't realize that it wasn't both of theirs."

"Mr. Green's condo is part of his business. He holds... I mean, he held his meeting here since the property house isn't conducive for signing contracts and such."

Mason was fair skinned, stocky, but well built, about five foot eight, who appeared to be in his fifties. Ann found out that he had worked for Mrs. Green ever since she took over as the CEO of the studio. He took care of the chores around the house for her, and Ann surmised from the way he spoke about Mrs. Green that he held her in high regard.

Ann and Mason continued talking while walking toward the unit. She found out that Mason had been a retired stunt double who needed to find work. Mrs. Green was looking for someone to help her since her new position was more demanding of her time. It was a perfect fit.

 Mason walked around the corner of the last building in the complex, climbed up five steps and inserted the key into the lock. He stepped aside and motioned for Ann to walk in. He handed her the keys and told her to just put them in the secure lock box when she was finished. Ann agreed and thanked him.

Ann stepped into the foyer and immediately saw the view of the harbor. It was a wide-open floor plan with the foyer spilling into the L- shaped living room. The dining room was outfitted with a long table, matching chairs, and a buffet cabinet. The color scheme was soft colors, mostly turquoise and peach. There were two bedrooms off a hallway that were to the left of the foyer, both overlooking the harbor. Turquoise and peach were all through the condo and had the look of being professionally decorated. There was a bar with two stools in the same turquoise and peach colors. Next to the bar was a wall switch. Ann flipped the switch. The fireplace lit up, the faux candles went on, and music started to play. Ann thought, *this is more like a bachelor's pad than a meeting place for business. The only business that went on here was monkey business.*

Ann was about to go to the bedroom when she heard a key go into the front door. It gave her pause and she stepped into the bathroom and waited. She heard the door open and close and heard faint footsteps heading in her direction. Ann stepped out of the bathroom back into the hallway and came face to face with Lisa Crane. Lisa jumped back, obviously startled, and said, "I didn't know anyone would be here."

"Why are you here?" Ann asked.

"I came by to pick up some stuff that I left here."

"How did you come to leave some of your things here?"

"Derek and I were seeing each other. He broke it off several months ago. I just never came back to get my things. Now that he is dead, I thought I would come by, but I didn't expect to run into anybody here."

Ann and Lisa continued talking about how she met Derek and her relationship with him. They had met when she was trying out for a bit when Derek was delivering something for the studio. They accidentally crossed paths as she was leaving. Derek stopped her and they started talking. He asked her to have dinner with him, and she had agreed. At dinner Derek told her that his wife was head of the studio and that maybe he could help her accelerate her career. From that night on and for several months to follow they were involved in a sexual relationship. Then one day, Derek abruptly ended the affair.

"Did Derek help accelerate your career?"

"No. Even though I kept trying out for bit parts."

Ann asked Lisa how much she knew about Derek's business. Lisa told her that he owned the property house, and from time to time, he would deliver certain props himself to the studio. That was all she really knew. Ann thought it was curious that Derek would deliver props and not the production property manager arranging what was needed. She made a mental note to tell Hank.

"May I go and get my stuff?"

"Yes. It is obvious that the police have not been here yet, or your things would have become part of evidence in his murder investigation. I don't see any harm in getting your things."

"Thanks."

Lisa walked into the guest bedroom, opened the closet door, and removed several pieces of clothing. She laid them on the bed, then walked around opening up the drawers of the single dresser that stood in the room. Lisa removed several cards, and several pieces of lingerie. She turned around and gave a long look at the closet where there were several remaining pieces of clothing hanging.

Ann pointed to the closet and asked Lisa, "Are those the reason that Derek ended your relationship?"

"I'm sure they are," Lisa said sarcastically.

Ann walked over to the closet and rifled through the remaining clothes. One of the dresses stood out to her. She had seen this dress before. At first she couldn't remember, then realized it was a dress that Courtney had been wearing in one of her interviews. *Hmm*, she thought, *I wonder if Lisa knows that it was Courtney's dress. I'm sure she does.*

"If you are wondering if I knew Courtney was seeing Derek, I did. Those dresses and such are Courtney's."

"Did Courtney know that you knew?"

"Yes. As a matter of fact, we talked about it. We worked it out, and I held no ill feelings toward her for her involvement with Derek. After all, we were both seeing Derek for the same reason."

Ann didn't believe that for a minute.

"You know, this puts you on the suspect list for her murder."

"I'm sure it does. That's why I didn't say anything to you and Detective Johnson about Derek and me."

"Lisa, that wasn't very smart. In fact, it was pretty stupid. You knew we would find out eventually. So, now it will look like you had something to hide."

"Well, of course I was hiding my relationship with Derek. I didn't want his wife to find out that we had been seeing each other. That could of, and would have, killed any career chances for me."

"I think it is time you take your things and go. I am sure Detective Johnson will want to talk to you further."

Lisa stuffed some things in a bag that she had brought and picked up the rest, carrying them out over her arm. She opened the front door, and before she stepped through it, she looked over her shoulder and shouted, "If you want to know more about Derek's business, talk to Stan Ritkowski." She left before Ann could ask her why.

Illusion, deception, things are not what they appear to be! Ann thought as she continued to search through the condo. *I should have known. The moon was this morning's card.*

CHAPTER 33

Ann left Derek's condo shortly after finding something very curious. She had found several articles of men's clothing that did not appear to be Derek's. They were in the main bedroom and were much smaller than the other clothing in the closet. From Ann's memory, she would have described Derek as a slender man, well built, around 210 lbs., who stood about six feet tall. The clothes she found seemed to be for a man somewhere around 175 lbs., and no taller than five foot ten.

Ann called Hank from the Empress. She got his voice mail and decided not to leave a message about her conversation with Lisa Crane or the clothing. Instead, she left a message just to call her. The next call she made was to Stan Ritkowski. Ann was surprised that Stan answered so quickly, or at all, since it was lunchtime.

"Hello."

"Mr. Ritkowski?"

"Yes."

"This is Ann Hart, the investigator in the Courtney Hill's murder case. I need to ask you a few more questions. Are you free this afternoon?"

"Yes, I was just about to step out for a bite to eat. How about my office in about an hour?"

"I'll be there."

After Stan hung up with Ann, he opened his desk drawer, pulled out a bologna and cheese sandwich. He had carefully made it that morning with three layers of alternating bologna and cheese slices. He leaned back in his chair, took a bite, and worried about why Ann wanted to talk to him.

After Ann hung up, she pulled into a fast-food drive through, got herself a salad and some iced tea. She pulled over, parked, and while eating her salad, wondered whose clothing she had found. The buzzing of her phone interrupted her thoughts, she grabbed her phone and said, "Hey, Cowboy, how's things going?" Hank filled her in on the case he was helping on, then queried Ann about her follow-up with Monica. She filled him in about the condo, Lisa, and the clothing she found in Derek's closet.

"Very interesting. It appears that Derek was a busy man. Drug trafficking, affairs with young and upcoming women, and maybe men, as well."

"Yes, what was a simple murder investigation has turned into a puzzle of characters. Even though we didn't ask Monica if she knew about Derek's side business, it will be interesting to hear what she has to say when I circle back to her. For now, I am on my way to follow-up on what Lisa said about Stan Ritkowski. I am meeting him in half an hour."

"Good luck. Who knows, he may be the mystery man in Derek's life. Got to go. Keep me informed."

Ann hung up, got rid of her trash, pulled out of the parking lot, and started out toward Stan Rutkowski's office. While Ann was driving, Stan was pacing. He was still pacing when he heard the elevator approaching his floor. He composed himself and waited for Ann to come through the door.

Ann exited the elevator and approached a door that had *Stan Ritkowski* in black lettering on a gold plate. She knocked twice, then opened the door. She just about toppled over Stan. In his nervousness, he crossed the room and opened the door even before Ann knocked.

"Thanks for being willing to see me."

"Of course. Come and sit down." He waved his hand indicating to sit on one of the chairs in front of his desk. Once seated, he said, "What did you want to talk to me about?"

"Derek Green?" Ann said.

"Derek Green?" Stan asked quizzically.

"Yes. Did you know him?"

"Vaguely. I know he owned the property house that the studio uses, however, I am not part of that side of the business."

"So, you don't know much about his business?"

"Not really, no."

Ann's internal dialogue kicked in. *He's lying. But why? He is up to his eyeballs in this mess. I know it..*

"Ms. Hart, are you okay? Did you hear me?

"Yes. Sorry, I was sorting something out in my mind. So, if you didn't know Derek Green, or as you put it, you knew him *vaguely*, then why do you think that Lisa Crane said that you did?"

Stan stopped talking. Ann could tell he was running scenarios around in his head. *Probably asking himself questions, trying to decide how much to say.*

"Mr. Ritkowski?"

"Yes, yes. Alright, I did know Derek."

"Why did you lie?"

"Because he was murdered. I just didn't want to get involved."

"Lisa indicated that you knew all about his business. Did you know about the drug trafficking part?" Ann asked.

Stan was noticeably surprised by that question. He squirmed a bit, wrung his hands. His actions were one of a guilty man. Ann asked the question again. This time Stan answered with a question.

"How would Lisa know about the drug trafficking business?" It was more of a thought spoken out loud. Ann didn't answer. She waited for Stan to say more. He continued, "Well, I helped Derek out with his accounting books."

"Did you tell the DEA about your involvement?" Ann asked.

"No one from the DEA ever came to see me," Stan answered.

Ann thought, *now I know why we have a drug problem in our country.*

"I am good at my job and since the drug shipments didn't come in all that often, I just posted each shipment as other merchandise to be used by the studios. Whatever came in as cash, Derek just kept. It was a good gig for him, until he got killed."

Ann realized she was talking to a man around six feet tall and about 175 lbs. She took a chance and asked, "Tell me what kind of relationship you had with Derek?"

"I just helped him out with his accounting from time to time. Nothing more than that."

Ann thought, *he is lying! It is written all over his body language.*

"Mr. Ritkowski, I don't believe you. I can invite you down to the station for more questioning, or you can elaborate about your relationship with Derek."

"I'm not sure what you mean or what you are insinuating."

"I'm not insinuating anything," Ann responded, although she had her suspicions and was hoping he would break down and tell all.

"I helped him out with his accounting," Stan answered.

Ann still did not believe him and decided to take a detour with her questioning.

"So, tell me Mr. Ritkowski, how did you get involved with Derek in the first place?"

"Through his wife, Monica. She knew I managed Stephen Knoll's finances and thought I could help her husband. She queried Stephen about me, and the rest is history. Derek was not good at keeping his finances in order. He used to do everything by hand and wrote transactions on those little sticky notes. They were everywhere. Once I learned about his business and got his books in order, he confided in me about the drug drops. Since I really wasn't part of the drug thing, I didn't see any harm in showing him how to incorporate the drops into his general merchandise."

"Didn't you realize that trafficking drugs, no matter how big or small, is illegal?"

"Of course, but like I said, I wasn't doing the trafficking."

"You are an accessory because you knew about what Derek was doing. But that is between you and the DEA. I'll let them sort it out with you. In the meantime, who do you think would want Derek dead?"

"No one that I know. I don't know the people who bring in the drugs."

Ann changed her questioning course once again and asked, "Did you know that Derek was having an affair with Courtney?"

"I came to know that he had affairs with a lot of people," Stan answered quickly with a bit of a sarcastic tone.

"Yes, I came to learn that as well. When you answered about Derek's affairs, you said people instead of women. Did you mean he saw men as well"?

"Yes."

"Stan, were you one of the people?"

"Wow, you go right for the juggler, don't you."

"I apologize. Sometimes tough questions need to be asked. Again, were you one of the people?"

"I am ashamed and embarrassed to say yes. It was a mistake and almost cost me my relationship."

"Care to explain?"

"Not really, but I know you will keep pushing until I do. So, here it is. It just happened. I had been at a studio party without my partner. I was ready to leave, but my car would not start. Derek was at the same function and offered to drive me home. Since it was late into the wee hours of the morning, I took him up on his offer. The alcohol kicked in, and one thing led to another. It was a one-time thing."

"Did you tell your partner what happened?"

"Well, no, but he did find out. Derek thought it would be smart to come clean to my partner and tell him that he took advantage of me. He thought that would get me off the hook. What a mess that became."

"Who is your partner?"

"Why is that important?"

"This is a murder investigation. Everyone that knew either Courtney Hill or Derek is important to the investigation."

"Bob Kerry."

"Bob Kerry, Stephen Knoll's manager?"

"Yes. The same Bob Kerry."

"Like I said, this is a murder investigation. I need to talk with everyone associated not only with Cortney Hill, but Derek Green as well."

Ann and Stan continued their question-and-answer session

for a while longer. Finally, Ann felt she gathered enough information for the time being. She told him she would be following up with Bob Kerry and the DEA.

CHAPTER 34

Ann groaned as she rolled over to check the clock on the nightstand.

"Shit," she popped up like a jack in the box.

"Why didn't my alarm go off?" Since no one answered, she shook her head trying to piece together the night before. Then it hit her.

"Oh right. The wine."

The night before had started out fine. She came home after interviewing Stan, poured herself a glass of wine, and called Bob Kerry to arrange to meet with him in the morning. He agreed. To celebrate, she had poured herself another glass of wine, pulled out her notes and started to go through them, page by page. That second glass of wine turned into a third and a fourth, until the bottle was empty. Ann had gotten so engrossed in her notes, and sorting out her conclusions, hunches, and ideas about the Courtney Hill murder case, she didn't realize how much time, or wine, had passed.

Oh, I remember now. The evening had gotten away from her, and in her wine stupor, she had forgotten to set the alarm. *Well, at least I woke up in time. I wouldn't want to* miss my *meeting with Bob Kerry. I have some very interesting questions for him.*

Ann jumped out of bed, dressing quickly before heading to the kitchen. She made her protein drink and while sipping it, she reached for her tarot deck. Ann pulled a card from her Tarot deck. Ann gasped. *It was the Tower card. Danger. Crisis. Sudden change. Destruction.* The Tower was never a good omen. She finished her drink and grabbed her jacket. *The Tower. Well, today just got a hell of a lot more interesting.*

Ann slid behind the wheel of the Empress and eased out of the garage. She decided instead of taking the main street to the studio, she opted for smaller side streets, avoiding the worst of the morning traffic.

She was mentally going through the questions she wanted to ask Bob Kerry when something caught her attention in the rearview mirror. It was a white van, traveling quite fast, coming up behind her. She thought, *I should pull over and let the van pass*. A white van. It was coming up fast.

Her instincts began to take over. Her logical part of her brain said it was nothing, just an impatient driver. But the way it was coming up and moving just didn't seem normal. Ann started looking for a place to pull over. *Damn. There are too many parked cars.* As she was deciding what to do, a black cargo van had stopped in the road ahead, blocking her path. She didn't see the second van until it was too late. Ann's heart started beating so hard she thought it was going to come out of her chest. She grabbed her phone and hit the speed dial for Deputy Huber. It seemed like an eternity for the call to connect.

"Huber, it's Ann. I'm being boxed in by two vans. A black van In front of me blocking the road and a white van behind me. I'm……" Before she could finish, she saw the side door of the black van slid open.

Two men got out. Their faces were covered by black knitted face masks that went over their entire heads. They moved quickly and with definite intention. Ann glanced in the rear-view mirror and realized that the white van was closing in on her. No time to think, Ann held tight to the steering wheel, threw the Empress in reverse, and slammed her foot down on the gas. *Okay, here we go.*

With the Empresses' tires screeching, she shot backward down the street, barely missing several parked cars. The white van saw her and tried to turn, but at the last second, she yanked the wheel, swerving around it. The white van started skidding trying to follow her.

Keep moving. Don't slow down. She reached an intersection and spun the wheel hard, turning onto a side street. She glanced in the rear-view mirror and saw the black van pulling back. The white van was still following her. *Don't slow down. Don't let them trap you again.*

At first Ann heard the sirens, then she saw the red and blue lights flashing in the rear-view mirror, reflecting off the buildings. She felt a sigh of relief. Ann slowed down and pulled over to the curb. Looking back, she saw two patrol cars flying towards the white vans. The black van tried to turn around, but it was too late. The cops were already there. *Huber came through.* She let out another sigh of relief. *Not today assholes, not today!*

When she saw Deputy Huber turn the corner towards her, tears just started coming down. He approached the Empress, opened her door and helped her out.

Wiping away her tears, she managed to say, "Thank you. Thank you. I almost froze, but then adrenaline kicked in and I just started driving backwards, swerving all over the place."

"That was pretty fast thinking. Are you all right?"

"Yes, I am a little shaken up, but I am okay."

"Well, we detained both vans. My deputies have all three men in custody and they're on the way to the station. Again, calling me was fast thinking."

"Deputy Huber, can you go with me to interview a possible suspect?"

"Of course. Detective Johnson told me that I am at your beck and call. Where to?"

Ann told him about Bob Kerry and that she was meeting him at the studio. He told her he knew where that was and that he would follow her there, just in case anymore van's show up. As Ann drove away, her thoughts went to the Tower card. *Hmm, I hope that is all the danger for today.*

CHAPTER 35

Bob Kerry's office was on the lot of the IRF studio. Since it was a small studio, the only security to get in was a code to open the iron gates. Ann punched in the numbers that Bob had given her, drove through the gates, and parked in the area marked for guests. She stepped out of her car and watched Deputy Huber drive through the gates. She was still shaken up and was glad that Huber was behind her. He parked next to her, got out and walked over to where Ann was standing.

"Are you alright?"

"I am now. After that episode with those vans, I feel more secure with you here," Ann said.

"Happy to help you," Deputy Huber responded.

Bob's office was in a small building tucked in behind, what looked like a warehouse. Ann knocked, although it appeared that they could have just walked in. Bob opened the door and seemed a bit taken back when he saw the deputy.

"Why did you bring the police? Am I under arrest for something?"

"I had a little experience with some men in vans on my way over here. I asked Deputy Huber to accompany me. You don't know anything about that, do you?" Ann asked.

"No, and I'm not sure what you are talking about or getting at," Bob answered.

"My bad. I should just come out and ask you directly. Did you send men after me to stop me from questioning you?" Ann asked.

"Absolutely not! Why would I do that?"

"Oh, I don't know. Maybe a little something about your partner being involved in drug trafficking," Ann answered sarcastically.

"You mean Stan?" Bob answered with a question.

"Yes, how many partners do you have?" Ann asked, again, somewhat sarcastically. Her morning episode left her a little short on patience.

"Stan was only taking care of Derek's books. Actually, he just updated Derek's accounting system from post-it notes to actual ledgers. Derek didn't understand how to use computers. Stan showed him how to work with ledger books and from time to time, he would check the books to make sure Derek was entering everything correctly. That's all!"

"That's enough. Any involvement at all makes him an accessory. That's the DEA's concern. My concern is who killed Courtney Hill and Derek Green."

"Stan and I have told you all we know about Courtney," Bob said.

"Well, that may be true, or not. I asked you once before, why were you and Stan arguing with Courtney at the yacht party?"

"We told you we weren't arguing," Bob answered.

"I believe you were. I think she had something on you and Stan and was threatening to blackmail you guys," Ann said.

"That's absurd!" Bob retorted.

"Really? If I had someone go over Mr. Knoll's business contracts, bank accounts, and accounting books, would they find everything in order?" Ann asked.

"What are you insinuating?" Bob asked sarcastically.

"I am not insinuating anything. I will come right out and say that I think you and Stan have had your fingers in Mr. Knoll's cookie jar. Courtney found out and threatened you and Stan, and that is what the argument was about at the yacht party."

"Again, that's absurd!"

"So, you wouldn't mind if Deputy Huber here requests a search warrant from a judge?" Ann asked.

"On what grounds?" Bob asked.

"On the grounds that Courtney Hill was murdered. On the grounds she was seen arguing with you and Stan at the yacht party. On the grounds that shortly thereafter, she was killed. That's what grounds," Ann said sharply. "Let's add that your partner was helping Derek Green with his drug accounting, and he is also dead."

Bob just stared at Ann with his mouth open. It was obvious he didn't know what to say. Even though he felt she knew about his and Stan's financial shenanigans, he wasn't about to confess. Knowing full well that Stan had the books in order. Well, the second set of books, he said, "Do what you have to do. This meeting is now over. Let yourselves out."

With that, Ann and Deputy Huber left and walked to Ann's car.

"So, what do you think?" Deputy Huber asked Ann.

"Not sure. I really don't have any evidence of them embezzling money, just a hunch. I felt from the first time we talked to Stan and Bob that something was going on. Maybe my gut is off this time. Or maybe it is the drug trafficking thing. Nope, something is fishy with those two."

"A lot of crimes have been solved on hunches. I say, follow you gut instinct," Deputy Huber answered.

Ann thought, *yes, a hunch and a tarot card.*

CHAPTER 36

I hate to admit I am actually looking forward to having a nice dinner with Hank tonight, Ann thought as she zipped up her dress. She decided to dress up for the evening, something she normally did not do. Ann is more of a jeans and casual top type of girl, but tonight was special. She needed mental respite, and Hank was the perfect refuge.

Just as Ann was finishing up, Hank rang her.

"I'm outside in front. Do you want me to come up?"

"No, I'm on my way down. See you in a minute."

Ann grabbed her wrap, locked the door, and took the elevator down to the first floor. She could see him in his Tahoe through the glass doors that held guard to the vestibule. He waved and got out of his car. Ann met him at the passenger's door, where he was standing holding the door open. He bowed and made a gesture like a doorman.

"Chivalry is not dead."

Ann chuckled and climbed up to the passenger seat realizing that a dress might have been a mistake. His car was much higher than her Empress.

"Don't know why you changed your mind about having a nice dinner and a real date, but I'll take it," Hank said.

"I'm a little surprised myself. I have had a hell of a week and believe it or not, have been looking forward to tonight."

"Deputy Huber told me what happened. I'm glad you are okay. You need a break from the Courtney Hill case, or I should say the Hill and Green case. From what he told me, it's gotten pretty intense. No more shop talk, only wine and fine food."

"I agree Where are we going?"

"Well, I know that you like Italian food, so I found us an Italian restaurant near here."

"A glass, or bottle, of Italian red sounds really good to me about now."

Just as she got her words out, Hank pulled the Tahoe over to the curb in front of a restaurant with a valet stand. A young man dressed in a white shirt, black vest, pants, and tie approached the driver's side. After Hank handed him the keys, he walked around to the passengers' side where Ann was being helped out of the car by another valet. She took Hank's arm.

"This evening has potential," he said.

Laughing she held onto Hank's arm while walking into the restaurant.

Once they were seated, Hank ordered a bottle of red wine and when it arrived, they made a toast to the evening. They kept their promise and didn't talk about the cases they were working on. As they were nibbling on the antipasto, a second bottle of wine appeared and once again, they toasted to the evening.

Hank told Ann all about his time growing up on the ranch. His dad wanted a cattle ranch, but his mom wanted chickens and cows. HIs dad conceded to one chicken coop, a few pigs and a couple of milk cows. One of his chores was to help his mom with the chickens and the milking of the few cows. There were hands to work with the cattle. Although, there was one part of ranching he did like and that was riding.

"The horse-riding detective." Ann said, chuckling. "I can see you now, chasing all the bad guys, gun in hand, shooting."

"Hey, I was a pretty good rider. I bet I could've given those old cowboys a run for their money."

"I bet you could have at that," Ann said in a more serious tone. She added, "I'm really glad I said yes to a dinner date. This evening has been so nice, just what the doctor ordered. My dinner was absolutely delicious. Thanks again for such a nice evening."

"I'm glad as well, and the evening isn't over. Dessert is in order."

"Really? I don't think I could eat another thing."

"Alright then. No dessert but some brandy will top off the dinner just right."

Ann agreed. Hank sipped his brandy thinking about how beautiful Ann looked. The waves in her red hair fell just right around her face like a picture frame. He had fallen in love with Ann the first time he saw her. Knowing how she feels about not getting involved in a serious relationship with anyone, he has never told her how he feels. Hank settled for the occasional burgers and beer lunches.

"Hank, thanks again for tonight. I think this is the first time I have allowed my mind to relax since I started working on the Courtney Hill case."

"I'm glad I could be a refuge for you tonight. I would like to be that more often in your life."

Then Hank took a chance.

"Do you think you will ever let me into your heart?"

"Oh, you are absolutely in my heart. I wouldn't be sitting here if you weren't in my heart," Ann answered. She knew full well what Hank meant. She had strong romantic feelings for him but had held them back. She feared once she opened that door, there would be no going back.

"Ann, you know what I mean. I won't push you. Let's just enjoy the rest of the evening."

"Hank, please continue to push. Maybe one of these times you will get through to me." She leaned over and gave him a kiss on his cheek.

"Thanks for that," Hank said softly. "It meant a lot."

They finished up their drinks, got up and waited outside for the Tahoe. Hank drove them back to Ann's condo and parked in front. He unbuckled his seat belt, released hers, leaned over and kissed her. To his surprise, she reciprocated. Afterwards, they sat just looking at each other enjoying the moment.

"It's late," Hank finally said.

He got out of the Tahoe, walked around to Ann's door, opened it, and helped her out. As she stood, Ann wrapped her arms around his neck, leaned into him, and kissed him. This time Hank reciprocated.

Without saying a word, Ann slipped her arm through his and walked toward the door of her building. He didn't resist. Once inside, they entered the elevator in silence. When it reached Ann's floor, she slipped her arm from his, opened the door to her condo, and took his hand and led him inside. She put her purse down, took off her wrap and turned toward Hank.

"Would you like to take off your jacket?"

Hank hesitated. He was feeling a little apprehensive because this was not a side of Ann he had ever seen before. In the two years he has known her, their personal time together mostly has been burgers and beer lunches.

He removed his jacket and walked toward her, wrapping his arms around her as he pulled her close. He kissed her once again.

And so, the romantic night began.

CHAPTER 37

Ann woke up to the smell of coffee. She opened her eyes slowly as the bright sunlight was shining through her window. She normally closed her shutters before going to bed. This plus the smell of coffee was definitely out of her norm. Ann rolled over, pushed the covers aside and as she was about to put her foot on the floor when Hank appeared with a full mug of coffee.

"I grabbed, what I suspect is your favorite mug." The mug had a picture of the Empress tarot card on it."

"Your guess was right."

Ann swung her legs over the side of the bed, planted her feet on the floor, and took the Empress mug from Hank's outstretched hand. She took too big of a sip and burned her lip a little.

"It's hot, be careful. Let's go into the other room and have our coffee. I think we need to talk."

Ann pulled on her sweats, followed him, still holding her Empress mug and licking her burnt lip. Hank sat down on her couch, and she sat down next to him. She took another sip of coffee more carefully this time.

"About last night....."

Ann interrupted him. "Last night was perfect. It was just what I needed." Then added, "You were what I needed."

Hank was taken aback. She always kept their relationship at the flirty level. There was strong chemistry between them, and he knew that she was aware of it. She had always been more emotionally disciplined than he was, until now. The door to a much more meaningful and romantic relationship had just opened, and he walked through it.

"So, now what? Was what happened after dinner a one-time thing, or..?" Hank asked.

Ann got up and walked into the kitchen, poured herself another cup of coffee and called out, "Do you want more coffee?"

"No, I'm good, thanks."

Ann walked back to the couch, sat down, and said, "I hope it wasn't a one-time thing. Just...I'm not sure if I want to talk about 'us' yet."

"I can live with that," Hank said. "For now."

Ann smiled, "Thanks."

"Breakfast?"

Ann answered by asking him if he would like one of her protein shakes. Although he was more of eggs and bacon kind of guy, he agreed to try one. They sat drinking their shakes talking about what's next in the Courtney Hill and Derek Green case. Hank was still on a special assignment but hoped to be back working with Ann soon.

"I think, after what happened this past week, you should continue having Deputy Huber accompany you."

"I agree."

"I think I am going to take today to sort some things out."

"Personal or professional?" Hank asked pushing the envelope.

"Well, I was talking about the case. Courtney Hill's killer has blended in with drug trafficking and possibly an unrelated murder of Mr. Green. I don't mind telling you I'm not any closer to knowing who killed Courtney. I have my suspicions, but not enough to go on. Instead, I think I have uncovered an embezzlement situation. Finding the border of this puzzle is challenging."

"I wish I could stay today to help you sort things out...all things, but I have to meet someone later this morning. I call you this evening."

"Okay," Ann responded..

Hank smiled and said, "Well, my shake is gone, and it is getting late. I need to get home and clean up if I'm to be on time. I'm glad this morning wasn't as awkward as it might have been."

"Cowboy, who says it wasn't awkward?" Ann said with a little laugh. She *had* felt a little awkward when she woke up. When Hank brought the coffee, she sipped it right away, so she didn't have to say anything. Then when she burnt her lip that distracted her long enough to go sit on the couch with him. Getting up to get more coffee, bought her more time before she had to jump into a conversation.

Hank smiled and said, "Talk you later, Red." He hugged her and left.

CHAPTER 38

Ann sat down at her desk, pulled out her deck of tarot cards and thought, *I can't wait to see what the cards have to say today.* She shuffled the deck a couple of times and cut the cards with her left hand into three piles. A ritual she did every time she worked with the cards, and she pulled out three cards. The first card she drew was the Ace of Cups. Aces in tarot represent new beginnings and opportunities worth celebrating, while Cups relate to our emotions and romantic situations. Having any of the Ace cards appear in a relationship reading can indicate a positive new beginning or an offer of some sort. The Ace of Cups indicates a deeper emotional bond.

The next card Ann drew was the Two of Cups. A picture of a man and woman facing each other each holding a cup. The meaning of this card is the beginning of a new romance or a well-balanced friendship. Ann said out loud to herself, "Well, after last night I think Hank and I are past the well-balanced friendship stage."

The third card she pulled was the Lovers card. From experience, she knew that the potential for a new relationship was strongest when the Ace of cups appeared alongside the Two of Cups or the Lovers. Here she got all three.

Again, she spoke out loud to herself, "So, there it is. I opened the door for this to happen, probably sometime during the second bottle of wine. I'm glad that it finally came out in the open. We have been flirting with each other for the last two years. Now, Ann, are you up for this?"

The conversation with herself was interrupted by the ringing of her phone. It was Deputy Huber telling her he had some news regarding the Hill case and asked her to stop by the station. Ann excitedly agreed. *There goes my day off.*

She jumped in the shower, got dressed, grabbed her bag, and left. When the elevator opened, she cautiously looked around the parking garage. Even though it was locked and secure, she was just a bit more careful since her incident with the van.

Ann drove the Empress through the gates. Instead of turning left toward the main street as she normally would, she turned right onto the side street. Still taking precautions, she made several unnecessary turns until she was comfortable enough that she wasn't followed. She drove down the ramp to the freeway and merged into the flow of traffic. She was feeling less anxious now and emotionally settled down.

She gave a sigh of relief when she pulled into the parking lot of the Sheriff's station. She walked into the station, and went straight to Deputy Huber's desk. He was walking back with a cup of coffee when he saw her.

"Would you like a cup?"

"No thanks," Ann replied.

"In that case, would you follow me to my desk? I want to show you something that I think you will find very interesting."

Ann followed him to his desk. He pulled up another chair and motioned for her to sit. After she sat down, he pulled his computer around so she could see the screen. She leaned forward to read the bulletin. It was about a small property house being raided by the DEA yesterday. They seized around four million dollars worth of heroin.

"The DEA has been looking into the small property houses scattered all through Los Angeles ever since you uncovered those horses at Green's place. They seized a small amount of heroin in another small property house in the valley, but this is pay dirt for the DEA. Now, I have something else to show you."

With that he brought up another screen that listed the corporate owners of said property house. President of the corporation was Monica Green.

"What? Monica Green?" Ann said, shocked.

"That was my response when I read the intel. Her husband was the sole owner of the property house where you found the carousel horses. Monica was not on any of the paperwork that would have shown her involvement with the business or the drugs. And take a look at this."

With that he clicked on another screen and brought up the information on the small property house in the valley where a small amount of cocaine was found. Ann looked at what popped up and she gasped.

"What? Lisa Crane? She's the one that ratted out Stan to me."

"Ratted out Stan?"

"Yes, when I was at Green's condo, she surprised me when she walked into the condo. She was there to pick up clothing that she had left during her affair with Green. While there, she suggested I talk to Stan about his business. Not quite sure why she decided to tell me that. I think some of it was revenge. When I did talk to Stan, he told me that he had suggested, strongly suggested, that Derek Green stop seeing her. He told Derek that she could turn him in to the DEA if she found out about the drugs. Or blackmail him."

"I'd say she blackmailed him. Let's check out if there are other names on the business," Deputy Huber added.

They continued to check out the information on the different property houses that had been raided. It appeared that Lisa Crane was the sole owner of the small one that was raided. Monica Green wasn't the only name listed on the property house where the DEA found the four million dollars worth of heroin. There were two other names as well, Derek Green and Hany Al Shariff.

"Well, this is truly interesting. Who to talk to first? I think I would like to start with Lisa Crane. She seems to be all over the place."

"She might be with the DEA. I'm sure they are talking with her after their raid. Let me see what I can find out for you."

"What about Monica Green and Hany Al Shariff?"

"I'm sure they are talking with them as well. They may all be guests of the DEA. I'll see what I can find out."

With that, he left Ann sitting at his desk. He walked into an office and made a call.

CHAPTER 39

"Special Agent Hayes here."

"Special Agent Hayes, this is Deputy Huber. I am assisting with a case that possibly involves several people you may be holding, Lisa Crane, Hany Al Shariff, and Monica Green."

"All of them have been here for questioning. However, they've all been released pending further investigation. Can I ask what kind of case you are working?"

"Of course. It is the murder case of the young starlet, Courtney Hill, and Derek Green."

"Derek Green..wasn't he the owner of the property house where agents found around 30 bags of heroin?"

"Yes, that's correct. Monica Green is his wife. Did the interrogation reveal anything that would be helpful in the case I am working?"

"Don't know off hand. If you want to come downtown, I can go over the notes from the agents that spoke to each of them. If you can make it this afternoon, I will be here. Just let me know what time and I will have a room ready."

"Thanks. I can be there around two with the investigator on the case."

"Got it."

Deputy Huber was glad to be of help to Detective Hank and Ann Hart. Up until now, he hadn't been assigned to anything as exciting as this case. Deputy Huber was hoping to make Detective someday and the Courtney Hill and Derek Green case could just propel him further down that path. He was secretly glad that Detective Jonson was assigned temporarily to another case. It gave him the chance to work with Ann and prove himself a worthy detective. He walked back to where he left Ann sitting.

"Ms. Hart, I spoke to Special Agent Hayes at the Drug Enforcement Agency at the downtown office. I was right. They were all questioned and released. We have been invited to come down to their office to go over the interrogation notes this afternoon. Are you up for that?"

"Yes, of course. What time this afternoon?"

"Our appointment is at two o'clock."

"Well, we have just enough time for me to buy you a hot dog. It's kind of a thing. I'll explain in the car."

Ann was grateful that Deputy Huber drove since the traffic going downtown could be brutal. Although riding in the squad car did feel a bit strange. They did stop for a hot dog at one of the local spots. Ann explained that she and Detective Johnson would frequently stop for a hot dog or hamburger on the way to, or on the way back, from an interview. A case ritual, if you will.

Deputy Huber thanked Ann for allowing him to be part of their case ritual. Ann laughed and said, "You are now officially part of the hot dog club."

"Honored" Huber said, tipping his cap. He felt honored just to be able to participate in the investigation of their case. While enroute, Ann received a call from Hank letting her know about the DEA busts. She chuckled and said that Deputy Huber had beaten him to the punch.

"Deputy Huber and I are actually on our way downtown to meet with Special Agent Hayes."

"I am glad that Huber is stepping up to the plate. I knew he would, if given a chance. He is a good guy. I also called to inform you that I may be back on the case sooner than I thought."

"Sounds good. Looking forward to that. I'll let you know what Deputy Huber and I find out. In the meantime, I will give you this nugget. Lisa Crane is the owner of one of the small prop houses that was raided."

"Very interesting. Well, you have always had your suspicions about her. Have to go now. Thank Huber for helping out. Talk to you later."

Ann relayed Detective Johnson's message to Deputy Huber. He nodded and smiled.

Deputy Huber pulled into the parking lot of the Drug Enforcement Agency building and took one of the guest parking places instead of one of the VIP spots. He felt the need to explain to Ann.

"I didn't park in the VIP spot since we may be here for quite a while. Don't want to tie up the spots."

"Very considerate. Not sure I would have thought about that."

They entered the building through the parking garage and were met by Agents assigned to screen people entering the building. Once through the screening process, they inquired where they could find Special Agent Hayes. They took the elevator to the fourth floor and immediately were greeted by a man identifying himself as Special Agent Hayes.

"I got a call from the agents downstairs to be on the lookout for a uniform and a nice-looking woman." He extended his hand to Deputy Huber and said, "Good afternoon, Deputy." Then he turned his attention toward Ann and said, "You must be the nice-looking woman."

Ann smiled and extended her hand and said, "I'm Ann Hart, the investigator on two murder cases. Thank you for allowing us to peruse the notes from the interrogations."

"Glad to help. I have arranged for a room for us down the hall. Follow me."

Ann thought to herself, *so this is what a DEA agency office looks like*. Sparse compared to the police stations that she has worked in and much quieter. Just a few phones ringing and no one yelling across the room. Special Agent Hayes opened a door to reveal several chairs and a round table that had several folders full of paper sitting on top.

"Take a seat and I will show you what our agents got from the three people that were brought in regarding the drug busts.

"Well, let's start with this folder. It is labeled Lisa Crane."

Ann opened the folder and started leafing through the papers. Then she came upon some of Lisa's answers.

"Take a look at this," she said, handing the papers to Deputy Huber and Special Agent Hayes. "When asked when she became the owner of said property house, she responded that it was gifted to her. Take a look at who gifted the prop house to her. Derek Green."

"I didn't know that you could gift a business to someone."

"I don't believe you can. If what she is saying is true, then I could see Derek setting her up in business. But why would he do that?" Ann asked.

Special Agent Hayes answered, "Maybe she had something on Mr. Green and was blackmailing him. We have, or had, him on drug trafficking through his place of business. Maybe she found out about his side hustle."

Deputy Huber nodded. "I think you are right. Ms. Hart found out that Lisa had an affair with Mr. Green. Maybe by setting her up in business, she would keep her mouth shut about his drug business."

Special Agent Hayes added, "It appears that Ms. Crane was telling the truth when she said she didn't know about any drugs coming into her business. Through some investigation, our agents found out that the African drum filled with heroin was to be dropped off at the property house owned by Monica Green and Hany Al Shariff. Apparently, the delivery service that drops off merchandise for several property houses around town, delivered it to the wrong one."

"Hmm, I would like to talk to Lisa Crane and dig deeper into this gifting of her business and bring up the subject of Courtney Hill's murder again. I believe she had something to do with Courtney's death, and maybe Derek Green's as well."

The three of them sat and finished going through the files. According to the notes, both Monica Green and Hany Al Shariff said they didn't even know their names were on business, let alone know anything about heroin. It was noted that Monica Green remembered that her husband had told her that he had opened a non-profit property house to provide support for a film school. She said that he was going to provide the props, or whatever else that was needed, to assist in the making of independent films.

What they didn't know was Derek Green purchased a small 2500 square foot warehouse to store some of the excess inventory from his property house. He saw this as an opportunity to create a non-profit to allow for more drug deliveries. He needed three signatures to submit to the state, so he put Hany Al Shariff and Monica Green's names on the document and forged their signatures.

He didn't know that he would be killed, and it would open up a whole can of worms.

CHAPTER 40

Deputy Huber drove Ann back to the station where Ann's car was parked. She was glad to be back in her own car and started toward her condo when she received a call from Hank.

"Hey Red, how did it go at the DEA office?"

"If you are free, I can tell you over dinner."

"Never free, but reasonable."

"Ha Ha.... you and your corny sayings. Dinner?"

"Sorry about my corny joke...just couldn't pass it up. Dinner sounds really good to me. Nice or casual?"

"Casual, let's save the nice for another night."

How about I meet you at the little diner around the corner from your condo?"

"See you there in about forty-five minutes."

Ann drove into her garage, parked the Empress, removed the keys, and got out of the car.

Stretching, she exclaimed, "It feels good to be standing after all that sitting." She walked out of the garage, turned the corner, and headed toward the diner. *She thought, I am really ready to relax, and Hank is the perfect one to relax with. Why, Ann, I think you are smitten.*

Hank spotted her coming towards him and thought, *she is so beautiful.* He waved at her, and she waved back. She picked up her step. When she reached him, to her surprise, she reached up to him and gave him a very loving hello kiss. It not only surprised her, but it surprised Hank as well. He had waited a long time for this kind of reception and couldn't be happier.

"Shall we go in?"

"Yes, I have a lot to tell you," Ann said.

"It sounds like a bottle of wine may be in order."

"Or two," she quipped.

They were escorted to a table in the rear that was just perfect for privacy.

"This table is perfect. It's like he knew we are newly in love."

"What? Is that what we are?" Ann queried.

"Well, I'd like to think so," Hank answered.

Before Ann could respond the waiter approached the table asking for a drink order. Hank ordered a bottle of red wine. He asked Ann if she was ready to order, and she nodded yes.

"A bottle of a red wine and two hamburgers, got it."

Hank poured two glasses of wine and said, "Ok I am all ears."

Ann filled Hank in about Lisa Crane owning a property house that she said Derek Green gave her. She went on to tell him that Lisa didn't know anything about a drug delivery, which the agents verified.

"What about Monica Green and Hany Al Sharif?" Before Ann could answer, he picked up his wine glass and said, "Let's toast."

Ann picked her glass up and said, "What shall we toast to?"

"Let's toast to us."

"This is supposed to be a casual dinner for debriefing."

"Ok, then let's toast to solving this case."

"Yes, and to us as well."

They clinked their glasses, toasted and she leaned over and gave him a kiss. Hank thought, *she must have had a hell of a day, two unprompted kisses.*

Ann continued telling Hank about the non-profit business that Derek Green had started and forged his wife's name and Hany Al Shariff's name on the paperwork.

"You know, I remember when interviewing Hany Al Shariff, he told us that his family had paid for his way here and supported him until he could get established. My intuition is gnawing at me about him. I'm just wondering if part of that getting established included drug trafficking."

"It sure could have. Drug trafficking brings in a lot of money. Funding Hany's trip to our country and getting him settled takes a lot of money. So, your gnawing is telling you something is off. I do appreciate your investigative skills and your intuitive skills as well. I'm sure it has been trying on you to have been going through this investigation practically alone." He continued as he poured more wine into Ann's glass.

"You've had quite a day. I am glad that Deputy Huber was with you to help out. I will be wrapping up the case I'm assisting on next week."

"Thank you. Deputy Huber has been a great help to me. Especially when he rescued me from those men in the vans. I meant to ask him if they were arrested."

"Let's stop talking shop and just enjoy the last of our wine."

That is exactly what they did. Ann and Hank just continued to enjoy their time together.

CHAPTER 41

Hank's mind was taken over by the thoughts of Ann. He was on the way to a station across town to help interrogate the last suspect in the case he had been working. *I have waited a long time for Ann to respond to my romantic gestures. She's quite a girl. She surprised me last night when she made the first romantic move several times. I hope I wasn't just her respite and that it was sincere. Oh, stop worrying, you sound like a silly fool. A silly fool that has fallen in love.*

Ann's mind wasn't doing much better. She sat at her desk overlooking the water, drinking her protein shake. Her tarot deck of cards was sitting in front of her along with a folder of her case notes. She was having trouble focusing on either. All she could think about was her feelings for Hank.

I can't believe I let my guard down and fell right in step with the emotions I was trying to keep in check. It has been fun playfully flirting with him. Now, it has become serious, because of me. I guess it's true, what the heart wants the heart wants, no matter what. Well, let's see what the day is going to bring.

Seven of Swords. Really, again? The Seven of Swords is the ultimate lying card. It represents dishonesty, deception, trickery, lies and manipulation. *I need to decide which person to talk to first, Lisa Crane, or Hany Al Shariff, or Monica Green. I guess it really doesn't matter, it appears that they are all up to their eyeballs in deception.*

Ann decided to call Deputy Huber to see if he was free to go with her to do some questioning.

"Of course. I just found out that the three men, that were chasing you, are now in custody with the DEA. Initial questioning revealed their connection to a drug trafficking operation."

"That makes sense. They are probably the same guys that I saw at Derek Green's prop house. I would like to follow up on that a little later. Right now, I have my sights on talking to Lisa Crane. When will you be able to meet me at her house?"

"I can leave the station now."

"Great, meet you there."

Ann rinsed out her glass, grabbed her sweater and her folder of notes, and headed out to talk with Lisa Crane, again.

In the meantime, at the DEA office downtown, three men sat in holding cells waiting to be interrogated by the agents. The detective agency transferred the three men to the DEA when they admitted to drug trafficking. Before they were transferred, they were arrested and booked for attempting to cause bodily harm to another person. One of the men broke down. He admitted that they had been ordered to 'take care of' the investigator that had found out about Derek Green's drug side hustle.

Ann and Deputy Huber reached Lisa Crane's property house at the same time.

"Good morning, once again, Ms. Hart. I have an update about the men who were chasing you. Before I left, I checked with the detectives that questioned them. They admitted that they were ordered to take care of you. They have been arrested and booked. More will be revealed from the questioning from the DEA agents."

"Thanks for the update. Ordered to 'take care of' me sounds like getting rid of me. Very scary. That was a close call. Thanks again for rescuing me. Well, are you ready to have a chat with Lisa Crane?"

"Yep. Let's go."

Deputy Huber and Ann walked up to the door of the property house which was already open. It was a small version of

Derek Green's prop house. It also was filled with all kinds of furniture, fake plants, ceramics, books, and anything else that could be seen in films.

"Hello?" Ann called out.

"Back here. I'm in the back."

Deputy Huber and Ann walked toward the sound of Lisa's voice, weaving through all the stuff. They spotted Lisa who appeared to be scrubbing something.

"Lisa, Deputy Huber and I would like to talk with you."

"If this is about the drugs they found at my place, I told the drug enforcement agents that I didn't know anything about that."

"You also told the agents that Derek Green gifted you this place. Please explain."

"Why? What difference does it make how I got this place?"

"Because it is part of the bigger picture. That picture being the murder of your friend, and the murder of Derek Green. So explain here, or Deputy Huber can take you down to the station and you can explain there. What will it be?"

"Okay. As you know, Derek and I had an affair. He started seeing Courtney and ended our relationship. I pitched such a fit, that he set me up in this business. He knew I was only getting small film parts. I guess he felt guilty since he promised to help me advance my career, and it never happened."

"How did he set you up with this place?"

"He knew the guy who owned this place was selling it and he made him an offer. When it came time to transfer ownership, he put my name as the owner. It was that simple."

"I don't think it was that simple. No one just gives a place of business to someone for pitching a fit, as you put it. I think it was something else."

"Like what? What are you insinuating?"

"Like you were blackmailing him. You knew about Dereks's involvement with drug trafficking. I believe you threatened to turn him in, if he didn't do something for you."

"So what if I did? I had something coming. I started the affair because of the promises he made to me. When he dumped me for Courtney, that was a real slap in my face. He got what he deserved."

"Did you kill him?"

"Of course not! There was no reason for me to do that."

"Did you have something to do with Courtney Hill's death?" Ann asked, directly.

"What? Why would I want to kill one of my best friends?"

"Maybe because she got all the breaks. And maybe because Derek dumped you for her. Jealousy is a strong motive for murder."

"Do I need to get a lawyer?"

"I don't know, do you? That's all for now. I have a hunch we will see you again. Detective Hank Johnson may want to have another talk with you. We'll stay in touch."

With that, Deputy Huber and Ann walked back through the prop house to where they parked.

Deputy Huber spoke up, "Wow, you were amazing in there. I thought for a moment she was actually going to tell us that she killed Courtney. She is hiding something."

"Thanks. I've just had this gnawing gut feeling all through this investigation about her. I agree with you that she is hiding something. Either she killed Courtney or is covering up for someone. I don't know. But I sure would like Hank to put a little more pressure on her when he gets back full time on this investigation."

CHAPTER 42

While Lisa Crane was answering questions for Ann and Deputy Huber, Charbel Berry, Carlos Karam and Tony Khoury were answering questions as well. Only they were answering questions for Special Agent Hayes. Ever since Hayes met Deputy Huber and Ann Hart, he had taken a special interest in their case. Especially when he found out that these three had tried to either kidnap Ann or harm her in some way.

These three men admitted to being the delivery service for the heroin to Derek Green's property house, as well as other businesses throughout the Los Angeles area. They also admitted to following Ann Hart as they were ordered to 'take care of' her. When asked by the police to explain 'take care of' her, they just said that they assumed to follow her, detain and scare her. The police didn't buy that story, and neither did Special Agent Hayes.

Special Agent Hayes asked Charbel Berry, "Where do you pick up the drugs that you deliver?"

"Somewhere out of town."

"Where?"

"Don't remember."

"It doesn't' matter where. You are already charged with a felony. Keep having amnesia and I will see to it you will have attempted murder added to drug trafficking charges."

"Ok. We pick up deliveries from an Afghanistan gift store in Los Angeles."

"How do you know when to pick up a delivery?"

"Tony Khoury gets a call letting us know that there is an item that needs to be delivered."

"Who calls Tony?"

"I really don't know. His name is Hany something or something Hany. I've just heard Tony on the phone with him."

Hayes ended the session with Berry and went on to question Carlos Karam and Tony Khoury. The answers corroborated each other's stories. Tony Khoury did give up the name of the man who called him when the pickup was ready. The man's name was Hany Al Shariff.

"Deputy Huber, this is Special Agent Hayes. I have some new for you."

"Thanks. What news?"

"I talked with the three guys that are involved with the drug trafficking with Derek Green. I took a special interest in them when I found out they meant to do harm to Ann Hart. They pick up the drugs from an Afghanistan gift shop when their connection calls them. Their connection is Hany Al Shariff."

"Hany Al Shariff?" Detective Hank Johnson and Investigator Ann Hart will be very grateful for this information."

"I hope this information helps in their Hill and Green case. These guys were all too willing to give up their connection. They are bozos playing in the drug trafficking world. They will have quite a while to ponder their ill-fated choices."

"Are your guys going after Hany Al Shariff?"

"They are out there now rounding him up. Will keep you informed."

"Thanks Hayes."

A few minutes later, Detective Hank Johnson walked into the station.

"Hey Hank, what are you doing here?" asked one of the deputies.

"The case that I was assisting on got wrapped up last night. Thought I'd stop by and check in with Deputy Huber."

"He's in the back, probably by the coffee pot."

Hank chuckled and continued walking through the station, high fiving the deputies that he passed. "I knew I'd find you back here."

"Hank, good to see you. Are you back for good?"

"Yep, at least for now. Can you bring me up to date on the Hill and Green case? I called Ann but her phone must be off."

"Of course." Deputy Huber brought Detective Hank

Johnson up to date about the Interview with Lisa Crane and the information from Special Agent Hayes.

"Does Ann know about Hany Al Shariff?"

"I don't think so. She knows that his name was on the property house that was raided, but she doesn't know that the DEA is going after him."

"How'd you like to take a ride?"

"Are you thinking about going to Hany Al Shariff's as well."

"Yes. You said that Ann doesn't know that the DEA is going after him. Knowing her, she is probably on her way to question him."

Deputy Huber and Detective Johnson jumped into the squad car and drove off toward the studio.

CHAPTER 43

After Ann left Deputy Huber at Lisa Crane's prop house, she decided to grab a quick salad and go see Hany Al Shariff at the studio. She wanted to find out why he was listed as one of the owners on the prop house. She didn't know his connection to the three men who had followed her. She pulled into a drive-through, got her salad, and parked. While sitting and eating her salad her mind started to go over her interview with Lisa Crane. *Something is missing.*

Driving to the studio, she was hoping that he would be there and not out scouting for Stephen Knoll. Ann arrived in record time and punched in the numbers that Bob Kerry had given her. She parked and walked towards Bob's office.

She knocked on Bob's door and was surprised that the door opened so quickly. Bob just happened to be on his way out and was getting ready to open the door when Ann knocked. They were both surprised by the encounter.

"Ms. Hart. What are you doing here?"

"I'm on my way to see Hany Al Shariff. Can you tell me where his office is located?"

"It is a little tricky finding his office as it is tucked inside the studio between sets. I'll be glad to take you."

He was right. It was difficult to find, and Ann was grateful for his help. Hany's office was really a makeshift space between sets. Ann thanked him, and he seemed relieved that she wasn't there to see him.

Hany's door was open. He was standing over his desk with papers in his hand and turned around when he heard Ann come in.

"Ms. Hart? What are you doing here?"

"That's the second time I have been asked that question. Bob Kerry just asked the same one. I'm here to see you. I want to talk to you about your name appearing as one of the owners on a property house that was raided by the DEA."

"Are you working with the DEA?"

"No, not really. As you know, I am working on the Courtney Hill and Derek Green murder case. But when I saw your name appear as one of the owners, I became curious and wanted to find out more."

"I was interviewed by the DEA about that. I will tell you the same thing that I told them. I didn't know why my name was on that business."

"Why do you think that Derek Green put your name on the property."

"I really don't know."

"How well did you know Derek Green."

"Not well. Met him here at the studio when he was delivering props."

"Did you know about his prop house being used for drug trafficking before the DEA interviewed you?"

"No, not really."

"Mr. Shariff, what do you mean, *not really*?"

"I really don't need to answer any questions by you. You don't work for the Drug Enforcement Administration, and they interrogated me on the same issue."

"You are right, I don't work with the DEA. However, Derek Green and Courtney Hill were murdered. You knew both of them. That makes you a suspect. Maybe you killed Courtney because she wouldn't go out with you...and.....maybe you killed Derek Green as well."

"How ridiculous! If I killed every woman who wouldn't go out with me....."

Hany Al Shariff was interrupted mid-sentence when agents from the Drug Enforcement Agency came into his office.

"Hany Al Shariff, you are under arrest for the crime of drug trafficking."

Ann stepped aside to the far side of the room with a look of surprise on her face. The same look that Hany Al Shariff had on his. One of the agents took Hany Al Shariff by the arm and turned him around. Another agent handcuffed his hands.

"What's going on here? I was just released by your agency."

"That was before your goons gave you up. Let's go."

As the agents were walking Hany Al Shariff out of his office, Detective Hank Johnson and Deputy Huber arrived. Ann stood in the middle of the office, wide eyed and finally asked, "What just happened here?"

"Come on, let's all grab a cup of coffee, and we will bring you up to date."

"Sounds good to me."

CHAPTER 44

Hany Al Shariff squirmed, talked in circles, and frustrated the agents interrogating him.

"Cut the crap. Your three buddies told us everything. We just want to know who your man is in the middle?" said the agent, losing his patience.

"I have no contact. I don't run the operation."

"Someone has to get the heroin into our country. Who ships it to you?"

"I'm not answering any more questions," Hany said.

"One more thing, did you have anything to do with the murders of either Courtney Hill or Derek Green?"

"I told you that I am not answering anymore questions."

"We will be questioning you more when your attorney shows up."

Detective Hank Johnson, Deputy Huber and Ann Hart gathered around a table at a coffee shop near the studio. Deputy Huber filled Ann in about the phone call from Special Agent Hayes. He told him that the three men, they were holding, mentioned Hany Al Shariff's name.

"Damn, I didn't see that one coming," Ann responded.

"I walked in right after his phone call and figured out that you must be on your way to talk with Shariff about his name being listed as one of the owners of the property house that was raided. We knew you didn't know about his involvement with the three men who followed you. Hany could have been the man who gave the order to 'take care of' you... To take you out."

"I shudder to think that they came so close," Ann said.

"You were lucky," Hank said.

"Yes, thanks to Deputy Huber. So, Hany was involved with Derek Green and his drug trafficking?" Ann asked.

"From what we understand, yes. He may be the boss."

"Well, this puts a whole new spin on this investigation. He could also be involved with the murder of Derek Green. Can you get us a warrant to search his office and his home? We may find something that will tie him to the murder."

"I'm sure the DEA has already got that covered."

"I'll call Special Agent Hayes and see if they have already done a search. We may be able to go in under the same warrant," Deputy Huber added.

"Great, in the meantime I'm starved. I grabbed a salad on my way down here, but I sure could use something more to eat. Anybody game for hamburgers?" Ann asked.

"Let's do it," Hank answered.

"You guys go ahead. I need to get back to the station."

Ann drove Hank to the station to pick up his car. She drove to her condo, parked and waited outside for him to pick her up. She was starving and mentally exhausted. *I'm so glad he is back on the case.*

CHAPTER 45

Deputy Huber and eight other law enforcement officers drove up the circular driveway, their squad cars crunching over the gravel as they approached the front of the house. Hany's home was one of the smaller mansions on the boulevard. It stood out and was known as the lime green mini mansion.

"Damn, who lives like this," one of the officers muttered.

"Apparently, drug traffickers," another replied.

"Or murderers," Huber added, stepping out of his car. He pulled up an image on his phone and turned the screen toward the group. "We're looking for a tool that looks something like this." He held up his phone with a picture of a tool that is used on yachts.

The picture displayed was a rigging knife, an essential tool for yachts. Detective Hank Johnson had gotten the lead from the man at the yacht yard, a guy with sandy blonde hair, who confirmed one was missing from the yacht. This is what we believe was the murder weapon that killed Courtney Hill as well as Derek Green.

"Got it," one of the officers said. "Let's go open some drawers."

They all moved into the house. Doors swung open, cabinets checked, boxes were yanked from shelves. Clothes hit the floor as closets were stripped.

"Hey, get a load of this."

"What is it?"

Huber turned around and looked at the officer who was holding a box.

"A bunch of newspapers. Looks like they are from the Middle East. I can't read Arabic or whatever language those papers are written in."

He rifled through the papers until his finger hit something hard. "Well, look what we have here. It's the rigging knife. I'm sure

this is the tool that we have been looking for."
"Why in the world would he keep this."
"Lucky for us he did."

this is a tool that we have been about
why in the world would he. Leaping
luck to us he did.

CHAPTER 46

"Damn, I should have talked to Hany Al Shariff sooner. Too busy focusing on 'hand in the cookie jar' crap. Who cares if Stan and Bob are pilfering money from Stephen. Courtney and Derek deserved more from me," Ann said, critically.

"Red, you are a bad ass investigator. Due to your illegal midnight caper you busted a heroin trafficking ring. Notwithstanding you almost became collateral damage."

"Thanks Cowboy. Although you didn't have to emphasize the illegal part. On another note, I just never considered Hany Al Shariff a serious suspect. I was more focused on Lisa Crane. I don't know. I still think she had something to do with the Courtney Hill's murder. I don't know about Derek Green, maybe she killed him too."

"Well, the deputies are searching Hany's place today. We should be hearing from Huber soon. We will know our next move depending on the results of that search. Until then, let's order our lunch."

"Don't you mean brunch?"

"Brunch, lunch...hey, whatever! Just so glad we got to hang out at your place so long this morning. It's been a long time since I've been able to do that...at my place or yours."

"And the night wasn't half bad either," Ann smiled, the memory still fresh in her mind. They had enjoyed a well-deserved, and much-needed, evening away from police work. They ate, drank and laughed their way through the evening, which ended in closeness and romance.

Halfway through their lunch Hank's phone buzzed. It was a text from Huber. He read it quickly, then turned the phone towards Ann.

Her eyes widened. "What? Could we really be that lucky?"

Hank nodded, slipping his phone back into his pocket.

"Let's finish up and head to the station. I have a plan. Tell you on the way."

Ann was too excited to eat another bite. She took a hurried sip of water, hoping to wash down what little she had left. Hank grabbed the check, handed his credit card to the cashier, and signed without a second glance. By the time he signed, Ann was already waiting outside, ready to go.

Ann and Hank entered the station's lot in record time.

"I thought we were going to take that corner on three tires."

Laughing, Hank said, "I think we did. Let's find Huber."

Entering the station several deputies greeted them.

"Huber has some great news for you guys," the deputy reported.

"We know, he texted us. Is he in the back?" Hank asked.

"Yes, coffee time, you know."

Deputy Huber came around the corner carrying a cup of coffee.

"Great job Huber. Let's talk. I have a plan."

CHAPTER 47

"Since you have connected with Special Agent Hayes, would you arrange to have Hany AL Shariff brought to the station. I want a crack at him. The DEA has him on drug trafficking and I want to nail him on a double homicide," Hank ordered.

"I will make it happen," Deputy Huber responded, confidently.

"Ann, can you call Lisa Crane and arrange for her to come to the station as well. I want to take a shot at her. I've never known your hunches to be wrong. I agree she is mixed up in these murders," Hank requested.

"Yes, of course," Ann said nodding.

It had been three months since Courtney Hill's body was caught in a net, and two months since Derek Green's body was dumped in an alley. Ann and Hank have worked on untangling the web of lies surrounding these murders. Now, rolling the dice, they feel these meetings may give them their answer.

The meetings were set. Special Agent Hayes and several other agents escorted Hany Al Shariff into the station. Deputies escorted them to one of the interrogation rooms. He was secured in the chair, left alone, and monitored through a one-way mirror. *So far so good. The first part of the plan was in place.*

Ann called Lisa requesting her presence at the station. She only told her that Detective Johnson wanted to talk with her to close up some loose ends. Lisa walked into the station, asked for Detective Johnson, and was escorted to another interrogation room. She was told that Detective Johnson would be in soon. She was being monitored through a one-way mirror, too.

Detective Hank Johnson walked into the room where Hany Al Shariff was sitting. Hanny stirred and tried to loosen the chains that were securing him.

"What the hell. Why am I here? I've already been charged by the DEA."

"Murder. Plain and simple. Murder."

"What?"

"I am accusing you of the murders of Courtney Hill and Derek Green."

"You're crazy. I discovered Courtney, why would I kill her?"

"Oh, maybe because she found out about your drug partnership with Derek Green. I think she was blackmailing you. Although, I'm not sure what her pay off was. Maybe it was the part in Stephen Knoll's film. And I think you knocked off Derek because Ann Hart accidently found out about the drugs. Derek was sloppy and allowed your men to be discovered by Ann."

"All circumstantial stuff. But I admire your persistence," Hany said.

With that, Hank's phone buzzed. It was a text from Huber letting him know that Lisa Crane was waiting in the interrogation room.

"Sorry, I have to step out. You sit there and just think about the circumstantial stuff while I'm gone."

Detective Johnson left the room, gave Deputy Huber a quick thumbs up and then entered the room where a very nervous Lisa Crane was sitting.

"Lisa, thanks for coming down. We are getting close to wrapping up the murder investigation. I just have a few loose ends that you may be able to tie up for us."

"You mean you know who killed Courtney?" Lisa asked, her voice cracking.

"We have a pretty good idea." Just then Hank's phone buzzed. It was a text from Deputy Huber.

"Sorry, I have to step out. Sit tight."

He left and gave Deputy Huber another thumbs up. Then went back into Hany's room.

"So, Hany, let's talk about that circumstantial stuff. We have evidence that you killed Courtney and Derek with a tool from the yacht. You saw Courtney on the lower deck after her ex-boyfriend brought her back to the boat. You saw that as your chance. You hid behind the shelf that held the small boat and jet skis, found a toolbox, and grabbed a sharp tool. When she climbed out of the boat, you watched her friend leave and saw your chance to get rid of her. You stabbed her and pushed her into the water."

"That's quite a story. You can't prove any of that."

"Yes, we can."

Just then Deputy Huber opened the door.

"We have an emergency out here and need you."

Hank got up and walked out leaving Hany Al Shariff wondering what evidence they had collected.

"The plan is working. He is ready to talk. I know it. Now back to Ms. Crane," Hank said confidently.

Hank walked back into Lisa's room. Her face was drawn, and her eyes seemed so hollow.

"Ok, where were we?"

"You said that you knew who killed Courtney."

"Yes and no. We thought you could help us sort things out."

"Me? How?" Lisa said, her voice cracking.

"Let me start by asking you some questions."

He started by asking some soft questions, then circled back and asked harder questions in a harsher way. Lisa kept fidgeting in the chair and playing with the cuticles on her fingers.

"You and your investigator have been hounding me and hounding me. Why?" Lisa asked looking like she was on the verge of tears.

"Well, we believe you had something to do with her murder. Her ex-boyfriend came in his boat and picked her up from the lower deck sometime during the party. He said that he saw someone standing next to Courtney and waited for that person to leave before he boated over to pick her up. I believe that person was you. You watched them leave and waited for them to come back. When Courtney got out of the boat, you waited for her ex-boyfriend to leave, and you killed her."

Just when Lisa was about to say something, Deputy Huber opened the door.

"We have an emergency out here and need you."

"Sorry, Lisa." Hank stood up and stepped out of the office.

"Looks like your plan is working! I'll pop back in and tell her you won't be much longer," Deputy Huber said.

"Yes, I think it is. Now for the final step with Hany."

Hank entered the room where he left Hany. He walked over and dropped a plastic bag on the table in front of Hany. It contained the rigging knife.

"The deputies found this in your house buried in a box of newspapers. We had it tested, her blood and your fingerprints are on the tool," Hank informed him.

Hany's face twitched, beads of sweat appeared on his forehead and his head dropped.

"Hany you're through," Hank said.

"Alright! Alright! I killed the bitch. You were right. She blackmailed me into convincing Stephen Knoll to give her a part in his movie. But you got one thing wrong. Yes, I saw her on the lower deck. She wasn't getting out of a boat. She was climbing out of the water. Looks like I'm not the only one that wanted her dead. And that stupid idiot, Derek, was also being blackmailed. You were also right about Derek. He just got careless and sloppy. He was going to get us caught. He had to go. He got us caught anyway." He was talking so fast that his words were tripping over his tongue.

"It's over Hany." With that Hank got up and left the room.

"Did you get all of that?" Hank asked Huber.

"Got it all," Huber answered.

When Hank walked back into Lisa's interrogation room, she was crying. She saw Hank and whispered, "I didn't mean to kill her. I just wanted her to feel helpless, for once."

"How did you make her feel helpless?" Hank asked.

"You were right. I saw the boat coming back from the upper deck. I ran back down to the lower deck and hid. I watched her get out of the boat laughing at Dan. She called him just a plaything. When he drove away, I came up behind her and hit her with a bottle. I was just so angry at her for treating him and others, including me, less than her. My anger just took over." The whole time she was talking, tears kept rolling down her cheeks. "I didn't mean to kill her. I didn't mean to kill her."

"You didn't kill her, Lisa." Hank said evenly. "But you left her for dead. When she came to and climbed back onto the yacht, Hany made sure she didn't get a second chance."

Lisa covered her face with her hands, her body shaking.

"Oh God," she whimpered. "I thought..."

"You thought that you got away with it," Hank finished.

Lisa sobbed. "I loved her. I hated her, but I loved her too. She was my best friend. And I killed her."

"No Lisa. You left her to die. Hany Al Shariff killed her, but you gave him the opportunity."

Hank texted Ann. Lisa watched as Ann Hart walked into the room with two deputies. Lisa didn't fight as the cuffs were placed on her wrists.

Hank and two deputies walked back into the room where Hany was being secured.

"You know that girl had no idea how the world really works," Hany said.

"Stand up, you are going away for a very long time, maybe forever," Hank said.

"Maybe, but Hollywood loves a comeback."

"Not you Hany."

He left the room and watched the deputies take him down the hall. The door closed and locked behind them.

Outside, Ann leaning against the wall with her arms crossed.

"So, that's it?"

"That's it. Lisa will be locked up, trying to find a way to deal with her guilt. Hany will just be locked up."

Ann tilted her head, looked up and asked, "Justice?"

"As close as we'll get," Hank said, nodding.

Ann looked down at her bag where her tarot cards were. She reached in and pulled out the deck and drew one. She smiled as she held the card up for Hank to see. The card was Justice.

ABOUT THE AUTHOR

Joyce Bennett-Hall is an Author, Writing Coach, Life Coach, Counselor, Speaker, and an Ordained Minister. She is a warm, insightful professional who has spent over thirty-five years gathering knowledge and human data about different cultures and human behavior.

Joyce has published several books; A true story about her and her husband titled, PROVIDENCE, a self-help book titled, DELIBERATE DECISIONS. Her latest fictional work is the City Dreams Series – BETTY: A Story of Big City Dreams, RUTH: A Story of Center Stage Dreams, and CAROL: A Story of Family Dreams.

She is accredited with DDiv (Doctor of Divinity in Spiritual Counseling), MDiv (Master of Divinity), BMsc (Bachelor of Metaphysical Sciences), Certification in Alcohol/Drug Counseling and Recovery Coaching as well as an Ordained Minister.

As a coach, teacher and speaker, Joyce helps people find their paths to successful living and happiness by assisting them in completing their goals and realizing their dreams. For more information visit Joyce's website - www.joycebennetthall.com

ABOUT THE ILLISTRATOR

Adriann Santer is a 28-year-old California-based illustrator and designer with over a decade of professional experience in the arts. Known for a playful yet refined style, Adriann's work combines strong composition with clean, expressive linework that brings each piece to life.

With a background in both traditional and digital media, Adriann has created artwork across a wide range of projects, from book covers to personal commissions. This cover design reflects her love for storytelling through imagery and thoughtful detail.

For more of Adriann's work—or to inquire about commissions—visit Instagram: @rogue_mythos.

BOOKS BY
JOYCE BENNETT-HALL

Books written by Joyce Bennett-Hall can be found by visiting her website, JoyceBennettHall.com and include:

Providence: A Story of Hope, Love and Diversity

Deliberate Decisions: A Simple Guide for Real Success

Betty: A Story of Big City Dreams

Ruth: A Story of Center Stage Dreams

Carol: A Story of Family Dreams

www.ingramcontent.com/pod-product-compliance
Lightning Source LLC
Chambersburg PA
CBHW072151170626
46813CB00004BA/1762